THERE WAS A TICKLE IN HER THROAT

A funny wiggly movement. After rubbing her neck with her fingers, Beverly closed the front door and headed for the kitchen. She couldn't remember when she had last drunk any liquid. Spotting a bottle of Cutty Sark on the kitchen counter, she went to fill her glass.

"Perhaps water would be better, but I need something to help me fall asleep." She slugged back a mouthful of the amber liquid. A slight burning washed down her gullet. "A few more gulps, and I won't have a care in the world." Her voice, thin and squeaky, barely rang in her ears.

Quickly, she slammed her glass down on the tile counter. Choking sounds erupted from her throat. She kept trying to swallow, but a wad of viscous matter forced its way into her mouth, and she spewed it out onto the counter. When she brought her hand up to wipe her mouth, she could feel something inching its way down her chin. Beverly captured the gyrating soft body and peered at it. *Larva.* She squeezed her fingers together, and the insect's juice stuck to her flesh. When she checked the counter, she could see that the white mass contained maggots, which were trying to dig into the stained grout.

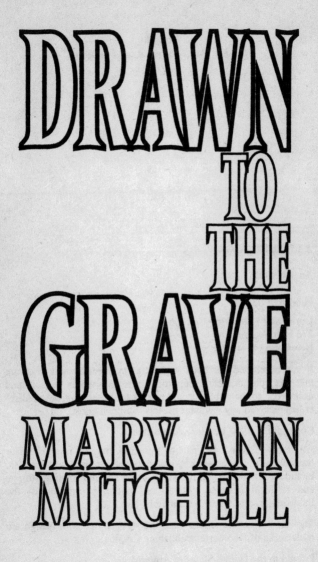

DRAWN TO THE GRAVE

MARY ANN MITCHELL

LEISURE BOOKS NEW YORK CITY

To John,
for his love, patience, and support.

A LEISURE BOOK®

August 1997

Published by

Dorchester Publishing Co., Inc.
276 Fifth Avenue
New York, NY 10001

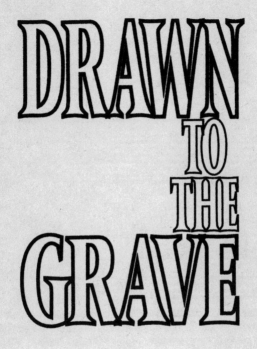

Prologue

She looked out the window and saw her own reflection backgrounded by the moonless night. Her olive flesh was creaseless in the distorted reflection. She pulled her auburn hair back, then heaved her curls atop her head. For several seconds she stood with her elbows bent outward at ear level.

Evan was quiet in the bedroom. He could sleep, but she couldn't. Beverly brought her arms down suddenly and watched her hair spew out into waves that rested finally upon her bare shoulders. Reflected in the window, her skin looked ephemeral, delicate, wispy. Age hadn't marred her beauty. Yet.

She had cried while they had made love that evening.

"What's wrong, Beverly?" he had asked. "Am I hurting you?"

She shook her head, and so did her reflection.

He had moved quickly to complete the act. He was obviously confused but didn't want to release her until he was finished. She had understood his needs but not her own.

Beverly turned away from the window. The room was almost empty. She was a minimalist: Her cream leather sofa was framed only by two standing lamps and a small Parsons table. At the opposite end of the long room were a butcher-block table and two folding chairs. Dirty glasses, dishes, and silverware were scattered across the table's surface. Their dinner together had been quiet. She had sat watching each of his movements. Evan's blond curls had spilled down onto his clear brow. Not a wrinkle or a blemish on that soft white skin, she thought. Evan's blue irises floated in perfect white; no tinge of yellow or rude redness intruded.

When she had first met Evan, she thought he looked too youthful to be at a late-night party. Underage. The wonder in his eyes as he observed the pretentiously chic people present in her apartment drew her to him.

"Hi, I came with Bill. Hope you don't mind," he had said upon catching her in mid-stare.

"No, of course not. Are you new in town?" she had inquired banally.

"I look that green? I was trying to look sophisticated, like I've been around these parties before. But you caught me. Only been in town a month now, staying with Bill." His voice had been steadily rising to meet the noisy challenge of other conversations and music.

She had nodded. Then she had drifted away from the cute little boy to talk with some grown-ups.

Later she had discovered he wasn't underage but nineteen, as Bill had clarified during some casual party talk. Bill happened to be Evan's father and one of Beverly's ex-lovers. Bill, naturally, wandered home with a blonde the night of the party, leaving Evan behind.

"I guess you can stay here. The couch isn't comfortable, but I do have a sleeping bag in the closet." Beverly had hurried away to fetch it. Upon returning to the living room, she had found no one.

"Must have gone home after all," she had mused. "Just as well. I'm not going to feel like seeing anyone in the morning. I certainly don't want to baby-sit Bill's progeny." She was too tired that night to return the sleeping bag to the closet. Instead, Beverly had dropped it in the middle of the floor and had headed for her bedroom. When she had switched the light on, she had found the boy spread out on her favorite side of the bed. Beverly had shaken him, but he had muttered that he was too tired to get up.

The sleeping bag still lay on the living-room floor, she had remembered, but why should she get evicted from her own bed? Besides, he was young, not yet a man; how dangerous could he be? Although they hadn't talked much, she had liked the youth and had liked lying beside him. She had pushed back his curls and had almost been tempted to kiss him on the forehead. Instead she had patted his head, had decided to remain in her clothes as he had remained in his, and had gone to sleep.

The morning following the party, she had woken to the smell of coffee and bacon. As she had been orienting herself, Evan's head had appeared sideways in the doorway. At this point she had freaked and screamed.

"Hey, it's me. I've got breakfast on the table, unless you'd rather have it in bed. But I didn't see any tray."

"I never have breakfast in bed and I never expect to see plucky little boys taking over my home."

"Gee, I'm sorry. I thought I'd do something nice for you, since you let me stay over last night."

"I was going to let you sleep on my living-room floor, not on my bed."

"You know, I was heading for the bathroom, and I guess I took a wrong turn. Ended up bumping into your bed and just kinda collapsed onto it."

She had sighed then, and again now as she glanced at the remains of last night's dinner.

Beverly moved across the living room toward the cluttered dinner table. She picked up the bottle of champagne from the floor. It still had about half a glass of brut in it. Beverly poured it into a clean water glass that she got from the kitchen. She decided to join Evan in bed but tripped over his Nikes as she started for the hall. The glass slipped easily from her hand and shattered near her feet. One of the slivers of glass lodged on the first joint of her big toe. She knelt on her undamaged leg and picked the glass out with her fingers. It was a large fragment of glass and left a long gouge. She limped into the bathroom. While Beverly washed her toe, her tears started to fall. Her eyes became so blurred with the salty wetness that she couldn't find the bandages. Angry, she knocked several bottles off a shelf in the medicine chest.

She waited in silence. Had she woken him? She heard no stirring from the bedroom. Evan slept soundly.

Beverly bent down to pick up the unbroken bottles from the floor but ended up sitting on the floor. It felt good to have the cold tiles against her warm flesh. She leaned back toward the tub, but suddenly jerked forward when she made contact. Gradually Beverly forced her back to accept the austere chill of the porcelain. She pulled her knees to her chest and gave way to her sobs.

"Hey, I don't mind you teaching my son a few tricks," Bill had told her that morning. "But remember, he's nineteen and you're thirty-five. Don't get any ideas about having him move in with you. The weekends are okay; it frees up my time. Just don't look at this as any long-term thing. I don't want my Evan getting confused." There had been a pause.

"I bet he takes after his old man in bed, huh?"

She hadn't answered Bill's question. She had been embarrassed. How could she have thought that no one knew? Evan had claimed to have told Bill that he stayed at a friend's house. Beverly wondered if they had shared stories about her.

Bill had chuckled when she didn't answer. Then she had laid the receiver back on the cradle. Stunned. That was the only way she could describe what she had felt immediately after their conversation.

Beverly reached for the toilet paper on the near wall and pulled several times until her hand held a large clump, then she ripped the paper off the roll. First she blew her nose into the paper to make her breathing easier. Next she used the dry parts to blot her cheeks. Her head rolled back and rested on the edge of the tub. When she heard her sigh, it surprised her. She hadn't planned the sigh. She also hadn't planned on feeling this way about her affair with Evan.

She recalled her first breakfast with Evan. He had talked about his childhood.

"I've lived in Thailand for ten years. My mom moved there after her marriage to Bill ended. She was real hurt, so she turned to religion.

12

Mom works as a missionary. Initially, the job got her mind off the mess she had left behind in the States, but now she does it to save souls," Evan had confided.

In future conversations Evan would expatiate on his travels. His knowledge of Asia and his naïveté intrigued her. Evan had never heard of certain movies, television shows, and public figures that were common topics among her crowd. Was it her age or cultural differences? Anyway, he was certainly a better conversationalist than Bill.

"I've always called my old man Bill," Evan had stated curtly.

"But why?" she had asked. "Isn't he your natural father, or is it a coincidence that you look so much like him?"

"He's my father. My mother's never been with any other man. She married him after her high-school graduation. Bill was a few years older and already on his way to becoming a successful lawyer. But Bill never knew how to treat a woman. He flitted from one bed to another, sometimes three times in one night. Whenever my mother said anything, he would blacken her eye."

"But you don't call him Dad."

"I don't respect him."

Later, Beverly would learn that the only reason Evan was staying with his father was financial. Evan was to start classes at Columbia University in the fall. His mother didn't have the cash to rent him an apartment, and his father refused to pay.

"He wanted me to come live with him. Said I needed to be near a man, thinks I've been coddled. Bill thinks I should learn to be aggressive," Evan had muttered.

Beverly smiled up at the bathroom ceiling. Aggressive. *Honey, you have no problem in that area, at least not with women*, she thought. She recalled the first night they had made love. Evan had acted especially boyish during the early part of the evening. She had giggled at his pranks. He had been irresistible as he leaned closer to show her a card trick. His white cotton shirt had touched her naked forearm. She had pressed her arm into his shirt to feel the warmth of his flesh. His heat on her skin had ignited her stomach and made her breathing shallow. He knew his timing and the signals. He had kissed her gently, dropped the cards, and had caressed the softness of her unfettered breasts through the pale, silk blouse.

Beverly stretched her legs out across the bathroom tile and looked down at her nude body. "You still look pretty decent, kid." While saying this she ran her palms down her slender thighs. Perhaps there was a tiny bulge at the top that hadn't existed ten years before, but all in all she was pleased with herself.

Tomorrow she would call her editor and let him know that she would be leaving town soon to work on her new novel. He had left many messages requesting a date for completion. It had already been several months since he had approved her proposal. The trip to the country had been postponed more than once, because she hadn't thought it was the right time: Either her work required her presence in New York, or her love life was going too well to leave. But now she knew that the time was right.

The hallway floor squeaked. She looked up at the doorway and saw Evan.

"What are you doing in here?" he asked.

"Picking up bottles."

While returning the bottles to the shelf, she glanced in the mirror and saw Evan watching her. Her nakedness smarted.

"But, Bev, your toe . . ."

"I was careless with a glass. The toe just needs some antiseptic." She also reached for gauze and tape.

"Skin like yours is too beautiful to mar." He knelt and kissed the bridge of her foot. After which, his tongue licked down toward her injured toe. Beverly pulled away.

"Let me doctor it up for you, Bev."

"No!"

Evan's eyes darkened.

"I'm a baby when it comes to my own blood. I never allow others to dress my wounds when I'm still capable of doing so. Otherwise, I keep waiting for the other person to make a misstep and hurt me. I'll take care of it."

Finished, she walked past him. He followed, but then turned back.

She got into bed and pulled the lace-trimmed sheet over her. A few of the blue hyacinths that Evan had brought her lay atop the pastel peach bed linen. Some had been crushed under the weight of the lovers' bodies. The rest lay upon the wood floor. Their scent still permeated the bedroom, competing with the odor of sex. The perfume of love.

She started to make a mental checklist of all the things she was going to do the next day. Evan and she were finished. No one could hold on to youth, although this boy had allowed her a brief fantasy.

Evan slid back into bed, into her arms, and she indulged herself like an alcoholic on her last bottle of booze.

Chapter 1
The Drawing

Beverly adjusted the jalousie on the living-room window in order to view Carl. Among his blond strands stood some conspicuous grays. The gray hairs were coarser, sturdier than the blond wisps that had carried him through his fifty years. He swept his callused hand through his locks and settled into his wicker chair.

"Carl, do you want something to drink?"

Carl waited for Beverly to come to the porch door, then shook his head. Beverly, dressed only in her underwear, walked out onto the porch and sat at his feet. The cold wooden planks touched her thighs and caused her shoulders to shiver.

"Night's creeping up on us," she said.

"I've got to go home."

"Stay, Carl, please. I'll make bouillabaisse and fresh garlic bread."

Carl shook his head. She knew he could see the river peeking out from behind the trees. His rowboat would be by the bank of the river. If he started rowing upstream now, he would be home before dark. He rubbed his hands together, then stretched his arms out wide. As he brought his hands down to his knees to rise, Beverly grabbed one hand.

"Do you love me?" she asked.

He looked at her without expression. With his free hand he reached into the pocket of his white trousers and pulled out a piece of paper. It was folded into a small square. Uninvited, she took the paper from his hand and unfolded it. There was her body, sketched out in pencil: her long legs, the slightly domed tummy with the pubic hair rising almost to her navel, the funnel-like breasts peaking in dark swirls, and the slender nape reaching up behind the earlobes. But it was the perfection of the facial features that gave her the confidence to smile up at him. He stood.

"Tomorrow?" she asked.

Carl shrugged and moved down the steps to the gravel path. She waved, but he never turned to see it. He would probably listen to some Mahler, she thought, finish the Nietzsche book that they had discussed earlier that day, and have a light supper.

Most of the next day Beverly pecked at letters

on her computer keyboard, forming words that ran into sentences. The drawing lay to the right of the keyboard. She was sorry she hadn't asked him to sign it, "Love, Carl." Maybe tonight.

Beverly had dinner late that night. She didn't know whether to make it for one or two. Eventually she put single portions on the stove. At bedtime she plumped up some pillows along his side of the bed and threw her left leg across the bottom pillow.

The pillow was still buried between her thighs when she felt a hand slide up her buttocks. She looked at the clock. Seven A.M. The hand felt rough against her. It coursed over her flesh like sandpaper leveling a rough board. His full lips touched her shoulder blades. Then she felt the hair of his chest rest softly against her back. She could feel her wetness spreading across the pillowcase as her pelvis pushed into it.

Later, at breakfast, she noticed how dark Carl's skin was, as if he had been working outdoors all the previous day. His blond hair had been whitened by the sun, almost camouflaging the grays. His hands were raw. Many calluses had broken open into wounds.

"You must have worked hard yesterday."

He didn't say anything.

"By the way, I'd like you to sign the drawing."

He looked at her and shook his head. His handsome features were pensive. She saw a cruelty that had never been there before.

"Why not?"

"I shouldn't have given it to you. I should have kept it for myself."

She smiled.

"I'm sure you can duplicate it." She started to remove her bathrobe. "I'll even pose for it."

Beverly dropped the robe over the back of her chair and stood.

"Let's go back to the bedroom and see if we can manage a repeat performance."

A few hours later, there were a blank paper and a pencil on the nightstand. On the bed Carl and Beverly lay entwined. She was awakened by the jolting movement of his body. Carl was trying to reach for the drawing material. Beverly moaned. Carl gave up his attempt and instead lay still beneath her. His breath halted a second or two and then slowly gained its rhythm. She waited. Ten minutes, a half hour, a day later, she didn't know which, then she suckled his teat. Beverly spread her legs across his hips and sat atop his body; she smiled, satisfied but hungry. He picked up the pencil and paper. Immediately she stood on the mattress and heaved her auburn hair up across her forearms. He sketched.

The drawing was not as perfect as the first. His hand was shaky, and the lines were not following her body contours. This seemed to anger him.

"I think it's good." She pecked him on the

cheek and got up to prepare lunch. As she left
the bedroom, she turned to look at Carl. His
hands obviously ached, for he grimaced as he
opened and closed his fists. He stopped only to
shred the paper and let the bits fall onto the
stained sheet.

Beverly retrieved her robe in the kitchen and
prepared an elaborate lunch. After setting the
table, she found Carl dressed and in her office
playing with the computer keyboard.

"You've got to turn it on if you want to produce anything." She giggled from the doorway.

She saw Carl glance at the drawing that she
had left next to the keyboard. Every curve, every
shading was in place.

"Come on, Carl. Lunch is on the table."

She was already seated when Carl entered the
dining room.

"Slowpoke," she teased.

At the table Beverly kept staring at his hands.

"How do you get those things?" She asked, a
forkful of pasta poised in front of her lips.

He looked at his cut and callused hands. "I
bury things."

"Bulbs?"

"What?"

"What do you bury? Are you planting a garden? God, it's been, what, eight months since
I've been at your place. Remember? It was the
day I signed the lease for this house."

Carl nodded.

"Can you imagine? We've been neighbors

now for eight months and lovers for seven of them."

Carl smiled at her.

"And it's been days since you smiled at me like that."

"I'm sorry, Beverly. I'm under some stress right now."

"Is that why you've been working so hard in the yard?"

He laughed. "As a matter of fact, that's exactly why I've been digging."

"You want to talk about it?"

"No!"

Beverly looked down at her plate and realized she couldn't finish the pasta.

"You're a special person," Carl said as he reached for her hands. He squeezed them tightly. "I have to go."

"Please, Carl. You never wanted to leave in the past. You would spend as long as a week with me and go home reluctantly to check on your place. Now I can't get you to spend a single day with me. Why?"

His eyes seemed to shimmer under salty tears that never fell. As he got up, she watched his linen suit fall in wrinkles around his robust body. He still had the body of his youth, and Beverly assumed it was due to his penchant for digging. She watched him walk to the threshold of the dining room and stop. His hands reached up and grasped the lintel. He hesitated. Beverly rushed from her seat and threw her arms around him. She could smell his body through the cloth, rich and heady, stifling her breath.

"I love you, Beverly, but . . ."

She waited for the "I can't make a commitment," which never came. He merely reached down to his right trousers pocket, almost slid his hand in, but stopped. Instead, he patted the pocket and pulled away from her.

Beverly watched him walk down the gravel path until he was hidden by the fir trees. When she brought her hands up to her face to rub away the tension, she smelled the garlic embedded in her fingertips and remembered that she had to clean the dining room after the half-eaten lunch.

After completing innumerable petty chores, she decided to hunker down to write. As she entered the office, she noticed that the drawing was missing. She searched the floor around the computer table, hoping that it had fallen. It was not there. Beverly sat on the hardwood floor and felt hot tears streaming down her cheeks.

That night, in bed, Beverly lay naked upon her cotton sheet, the tan of her body emphasized by the white of the material. Her dark eyes penetrated the dimness of the moon-sprayed room. The ceiling fan whooshed the air above her head, and her mind settled on that sound for comfort as she closed her eyes. Whoosh . . . whoosh. It became a lullaby amid the hyacinth smell of night. Beverly's limbs softened on the verge of sleep, when suddenly her breath halted and she found herself panting for air as her head turned toward the open French doors leading to the garden. She swallowed and choked, then with her hands she pushed her body up off the bed, scrambling to the floor. Finally, she was able to stand and move to the garden.

The summer heat, cooled by the moon's full glow, hugged her body. Her breasts, stimulated by the night chill, ached as she sucked in deep breaths of air. *A dream*, she said to herself as her breath started to come again. *A dream, a nightmare*, she thought.

But sleep never came that night, and it seemed that over the next few days she dozed lightly only at the keyboard or while reading on the garden swing. Deep, dreamy, reviving sleep never came. Neither did Carl.

One morning after her shower Beverly stood in front of the full-length mirror that hung behind the door to her bedroom. She had been skipping meals, and when she did sit to eat she barely touched her food. However, her body seemed to be swelling. There was a gnawing inside her gut, a steady nibbling at her intestines. As she belched, she tried to push on her stomach. Then she noticed the nail on her right index finger was loose—not just a portion of it, but the entire nail was coming free of its bed. She swung the bedroom door open and rushed to the bathroom for a bandage.

"Shit," she complained and wound the strip tightly around the finger.

When she looked in the mirror, she saw two reddish, bloated cheeks beneath the dark semicircles that sagged under her big eyes.

She had been pondering the possibility of an allergy or asthma, but these new symptoms frightened her. Could her ailment be more severe? If Carl did not come today, she would have to try to reach him. He had no telephone and no road led to his house, but she knew if she just kept walking upstream along the water's edge she would reach his place. But she didn't have to, because at midday, as the sun was peaking, he arrived.

He looked refreshed and even smiled when he saw her. Beverly moved awkwardly toward him as he entered her house. Her body felt full; her skin was pigmented with splotches of dusky red tint. A stale, eggish odor emanated from the folds of her flesh.

"Oh, Carl, I need you."

Carl held her and swept his long fingers through her thinning hair.

"I don't know what's happening to me. It started the day you left. I've had trouble breathing and—"

Carl pressed his lips to her mouth and thanked her.

"What for?" she asked, moving her head back slightly so she could see him.

"For what you're doing."

"I don't understand, Carl."

He moved her back through the hallway to

her bedroom and sat her on the bed. He knelt before her and undid the buttons on the front of her dress. His hands caressed her shrunken breasts and his tongue circled the hardened tips. Beverly was embarrassed, amazed, and soothed. Carl pulled the dress completely open and let his lips slide down to kiss her distended stomach as if she were pregnant from his seed.

"Do you know what's wrong with me?" she asked.

He nodded.

"You've taken my place in the grave, Beverly."

"What are you talking about?" Her voice was louder than she meant it to be.

"I'm so afraid of dying, Beverly. I'm afraid of the brown earth encasing me, swallowing me. Several years ago, when I found out that I was terminally ill, I traveled the Amazon, where I learned a trick, a means to stay alive, from a small tribe that lived in the dense rain forest. To forestall death, the tribal headman would carve out an exact replica of someone in an enemy village. Then he would personally bury the reproduction deep in the soil. The deeper he buried it, the longer the spell would last. At times, it's lasted as long as fifteen months for me."

"My God! What are you talking about?"

"The drawing, Beverly. I buried it after I left here last time—I had to do it. I could feel the maggots starting to eat away at my innards. I would have bloated like you and—"

Beverly screamed and grabbed her stomach with her hands. Her shoulders hunched upward as her body tilted forward to release a hoarse cry. Carl held her tight and kissed the auburn hair already lying rootless on top of her head.

"I love you, Beverly. That's why I almost gave you the drawing. But it was too late for me to find someone else. Neurological control had dissipated in my hands to the point that I couldn't draw a straight line—and it had to be created by my hands. A photograph wouldn't do. The original drawing was made when we first slept together. Then I didn't mind the idea of using you, but later it preyed on my conscience. I thought of how I would miss you—but this is the greatest act of love you could give me, and I realize you've always been braver than I. Probably loved me more, too."

"Carl, stop it. Why are you telling me this stupid story?"

"Because I thought that if you knew the truth you'd allow me to help. I can make your passing gentler."

"Passing? Are you saying I'm dying?"

"Oh, no, Beverly. You are dead. Now the decay starts."

"I don't believe you. How could you make light of my illness?"

"Beverly, you are beyond illness. Look at your hands."

She spread her fingers in front of her face. There was a black cast to her right thumb. Was

27

it a bruise? she wondered. Her touch did not cause pain, but the skin began to scale. And what of the roil inside her body? Her hands returned to her stomach.

"What about me, Carl? What about my life?"

"I'll always think of you, Beverly. When the time comes to take your remains down to the river, I promise to pray for you. I built an elaborate casket for your image. It's sturdy; it should hold up for quite some time. It'll make the decay take place more slowly. Give you time to settle any matters you think are important."

"What if I go to the police?"

"And say what?"

Beverly swung her body down across the mattress and rolled over onto her right side while still clutching the churning life in her stomach.

"I lined the casket with the best white satin I could obtain and smoothed the drawing across the bottom among some rose petals. Before closing the lid, I kissed your image, and I sang a hymn as I lowered the coffin into the grave. It was a moving ceremony, really. This is the first time I've ever buried someone I loved."

Beverly was screaming. Was it inside her head or coming up through her body? She was too confused to know for sure. Carl rolled her over onto her back, and she felt him trying to enter her. Her hands beat against his head. She pounded and kicked to release herself from this bringer of death.

From far away she heard him say that he was leaving; he couldn't stand to see her like this.

"You did it! You did it!" she yelled and watched him walk out of the room.

She slid off the bed and stumbled into her office. Alone in the house now, she sat at her desk, remembering every detail of Carl's face and form. She tried to duplicate him on paper but failed. If only her hands could mirror the image in her mind. All she could see were the pronounced cheekbones, the straight, slender nose . . .

What the hell am I doing believing this crap? She flung the paper and pencil on the floor. She needed medical help, not ridiculous voodoo.

She wrung her hands together, and as she did sheafs of skin dropped onto the desk blotter. Her howling reached as far as Carl, who was about to push his boat into the river.

Chapter 2
At the Grave

Carl ran his boat into the water and jumped inside. The cuffs of his trousers were wet. He had been in too much of a hurry to roll them up. He was thankful that he had left his shoes in the rowboat, where they now lay behind him, dry. The oars lay across the bottom of the boat. Carl looked up toward her house and heard the scream. She was angry, wanted more than he could give, and yet she refused the tokens he offered as lover and friend. No understanding from this woman, who had wrapped her legs around his body and promised to be his eternally. Now she was, but she spoiled it with her anger.

Suddenly Carl realized his shoulders were slouching. He arched his back and threw forward his chest muscles. Feeling better already, he breathed in the moistness of the river air and exhaled all that had rotted within him. At last the oars were in his callused hands. The steady splash that they made as they hit water set a rhythm. He was a machine, steaming through the steely glare of daylight, pushing through his life to maintain the vigor that belonged to him.

Swiftly he rowed. The sun at its zenith caused him to perspire profusely, yet he enjoyed the reprieve from the tension. Water splashed against the sides of the boat. His arms were not as stiff as they had been. He was rowing farther and farther away from his grave. His eyes sparkled with an unsmiled grin. Life was awaiting Carl just up the river.

The chimney of his house came into view. He could almost feel the cold cushion of his wingback underneath him. *Better than this sunheated wood plank,* he thought as he looked down at the knotted board upon which he sat.

When he reached his landing, Carl lifted the boat onto a dry patch of grass and covered it with a tarp. As he wound around the path to the door of his house, he detoured briefly to check Beverly's grave. The petunias and daisies were still fresh, and the mound was untouched. Satisfied, Carl returned to the path and continued on up to the house.

After running a warm bath, Carl stripped naked. He stood in front of a full-length mirror that was attached to the back of the bathroom door. His chest was well-tanned, with only a hint of a burn across the shoulders. The muscles of his arms were taut from the workout of rowing up the river. The stomach muscles were flat and his hips were still narrow like an adolescent's, but the tumescence of his manhood was definitely fully matured. His thick thighs spread farther apart as he appreciated the reflection before him. Already he could feel the organs rejuvenate, while his muscles and skin bulged with Beverly's gift of life.

Carl's slender feet padded across the small, round bathroom tiles to the tub. He dipped one bulbous toe into the water. Too hot. After adding some cold water, he re-tested. Perfect. Each foot plunged into the water in its turn. Carl issued a breathy sigh as he lowered himself into the tub. The water almost poured over the edge. When it steadied, he noticed the water was still a half-inch below the top of the tub. He wasn't going to worry about it, for he could always mop it up later.

Carl grabbed a bar of his homemade lye soap from the stool at the head of the tub and started scrubbing his body, massaging new life into flesh that once had been nearly putrid. He used a terry washcloth to skim off layers of old epidermis, to be replaced by the pink shine of fresh skin.

After a good forty-five minutes of preening himself in the bathroom, Carl moved into the bedroom to slip on fresh jeans. As he slid the denim over his hips, he saw a photograph of

Beverly on the nightstand. *Damn good-looking woman*, he thought, blocking from his mind the vision of how she last had looked. He picked up the frame and forced the photograph out, laying the frame back facedown on the nightstand.

With photo in hand, Carl moved to the study, where he opened a leather-bound album. He flipped through several pages of pretty and stunning women. No ugly ducklings. Finally, on a dated page he glued four black fasteners and poked a corner of the photo into each one. He waved an index finger across Beverly's form and remembered how warm and receptive her body had been. No more, unfortunately. Never mind, he thought, celibacy would help heal his still-warm frame.

Carl had kept photographs of all the sacrificial women, but hardly ever looked at them. He had learned how to move on, not love. Although Beverly had been different. The god had almost sacrificed himself for the lamb, he thought. Then he shook himself. He was no god, and she was no lamb. A pleasant woman, easygoing, insatiable, he thought with a chuckle. Often she was quite brilliant during their conversations, too opinionated sometimes. However, she had loved him, no doubt about it. She should have allowed him to make love to her one last time during the transition while she was giving her ultimate for love, he thought. Carl imagined the sexual pull of this love, taking from him the source of his life-giving power while allowing her own life to flow out to him. *Damn that woman!* he cursed as he slammed his fist down atop her photograph.

A chill swept through his body. Carl closed the album with a thud and exited the study, walking toward the front door. When he opened the door, he noticed that the sun was setting. He moved back to the hall closet and grabbed a flashlight before leaving the house. Carl followed the path midway, then swung off the dirt to plod through high grass. In the distance, he could see the mound with the flowers. The daisies were starting to wilt on the edges. The petunias were sturdier.

"I'm sorry," he whispered. His vision was blurry. Carl ran his right forearm across his eyes. He had never been so drawn to a grave before. He kept having to inspect it, make sure it was in place, that he really had done it. Carl had hesitated so dangerously long before he had buried the drawing that he needed reassurance.

"I loved you, Beverly, maybe not enough, but I did love—"

The daisies died before his eyes. They turned into scrawny stems with brown ashes at the tips.

He sucked in air. He was going to be sick. The acid from his stomach was gurgling up his esophagus. Carl bent over and held his stomach, trying to breathe deeply. It was no use; the force was too great. His day's intake spewed out at the foot of the grave.

Afterward, Carl stood tall, his mouth rancid, sweat dripping into his eyes, and his nostrils flaring.

"Beverly, Beverly, Beverly." The name echoed in the wood and haunted the river.

Carl looked down at his naked upper torso and wondered at the fullness of his flesh. Visually he followed a protruding vein from his wrist to the crook of his arm. Using a thumb, he pressed down on the midpoint of the vein, stopping the flow of blood; then he released it and marveled at the rush of liquid.

He sat on the ground, weeds almost hiding him except for the silver of his hair, which glowed in the oncoming twilight. Should he spend the night here? he wondered. This grave was different from the previous ones. Yet he wasn't sure why. It wasn't just his feelings for her. No, there was something reaching for him here, waiting for him. Carl looked at the grave. The petunias were still whole, the dirt under them dry.

Carl had made a marker in the shape of a cross. It swayed a little in the evening breeze. He thought about designing more of a memorial to her. Perhaps he would plant seed, bring fresh flowers. . . . Yet none of this would happen, he knew. They were always forgotten. Carl couldn't remember where he had buried the earlier ones. However, Beverly was different. He would care for her grave.

That first night filled with knowledge would

be the worst for her. Later she would resign herself. Maybe if he spent the night there, it would help. Perhaps she would sense his presence near her grave, enabling her to draw strength from his love.

Night had settled across Carl and the grave. He switched on the flashlight and shone it across the mound. Petunias huddled against the night chill, dried-out daisies waited to be blown across the soil, parched earth covering life, and a bent wooden cross waited to break apart in the first storm.

As he held the flashlight in his right hand, Carl used his left hand to rub down the gooseflesh cropping up on the opposite arm. He stood. To stay out in this chill all night would be hazardous. What if he caught pneumonia? He certainly didn't want to be ill during the first flush of his resurrection.

Against his will, Carl was drawn closer to the grave. He squatted down to touch the mound and say good night to Beverly and thought the earth had moved, but he noticed that the petunias and dust from the daisies were untouched. With his right hand he dug into the soil. If only he could touch her to give solace and say he was there. The hand went deeper into the loosely packed soil, feeling the tiny pebbles and twigs mingled with the dirt.

His tan face paled and his mouth dropped open in a silent scream, for a hand was touching his, fingers were intermingled with his own. Soft, slender fingers stroked the knuckles of his callused hand. Quickly he withdrew, feeling the other hand weaken and fall away.

Leaping to his feet, he flashed the light on the grave. No movement. No life. Just a bundle of petunias and rotted daisies. Carl brought his hand into the light, turning his hand back and forth, seeing nothing but dirt-clotted finger-nails, calluses, and dirty joints. Relieved, he reached up with that hand to sweep back strands of hair from his forehead. As the hand rose, a smell overtook him. Hyacinths. Beverly had always loved the flower. They grew in her yard, not his. He covered the area with a blaze of light. No sign of the hyacinths there. Again he brought his hand to his nostrils. Hyacinths.

This all could be an illusion, he thought. To make sure, he would go out to her place the next day. She shouldn't go too fast, or he would need a replacement sooner than planned, and as of now he had no potentials.

Carl used his bare foot to kick the rotted dai-sies and still-fresh petunias off the mound. He placed the flashlight on the ground beside him and pulled out the cross, broke the sticks across his knee, and flung them into the surrounding bushes.

One last look at the grave. He knew that by winter it would be hard to find.

Carl scooped up the flashlight and headed

back to the path leading to the house. Once inside, he would go through his bathing procedure all over again. Not a hint of Beverly would remain this time, he swore.

Chapter 3
Neither Living Nor Dead

When Beverly had first moved into the house, she had deemed not having a telephone an advantage. No temptation to call friends and chat for lengthy periods of time. She would be unable to casually invite friends for a visit without the sobering boat ride to town with Carl. Now the lack of a telephone and her lack of transportation endangered her life.

Beverly sat at her desk, staring out the window. If she followed the winding bank of the river, she would eventually reach town. But her cries and tantrums had exhausted her. Hints of dusk were starting to shadow the landscape. Would she be able to make it to town before dark? Probably not, and she would face the risk of falling and not having the energy to keep going.

Her office was a mess: papers scattered across her desk, writing utensils tossed to the floor, the wastebasket toppled by a kick. The childish hysteria hadn't solved any of her problems. She sat and contemplated taking a nap before she started out. Dawn, she thought. That would give her an entire day to march to town and would even allow short rest stops to regain her strength.

She slid her chair back on its rickety rollers and stood. Beverly walked through the house to the covered front porch and opened the door. Indeed, tomorrow she would take the dusty path down to the river. She studied the trees that obliterated the sight of the water. The leaves moved languidly in the summer zephyrs. The branches had been naked the previous winter, weighted down with snow at times or whipped by merciless winds that had broken some loose from their limbs. The trees had appeared to be dead, decaying. But the healing balm of spring had restored their hidden life.

"Carl, why did you lie to me? Why didn't you help me?" Teardrops blurred her vision.

There was a tickle in her throat. A funny wiggly movement. After rubbing her neck with her fingers, she closed the front door and headed for the kitchen. She couldn't remember when she had last drunk any liquid. With a glass of water she sat at the table. Somehow she didn't have a taste for tap water. She emptied her glass into the bonsai rosemary plant on the table. As soon as she had, her throat itched far more than before. Spotting a bottle of Cutty Sark on the kitchen counter, she rose to refill her glass. This time she stopped pouring when the glass was half full.

"Perhaps water would be better, but I need something to help me fall asleep." She slugged back a mouthful of the amber liquid. A slight burning washed down her gullet. "A few more gulps, and I won't have a care in the world." Her voice, thin and squeaky, barely rang in her ears.

Quickly she slammed her glass down on the tile counter. Choking sounds erupted from her throat. She kept trying to swallow, but a wad of viscous matter forced its way into her mouth, and she spewed it out onto the counter. When she brought her hand up to wipe her mouth, she could feel something inching its way down her chin. Beverly captured the gyrating soft body and peered at it. *Larva.* She squeezed her fingers together, and the insect's juice stuck to her flesh. When she checked the counter, she could see that the white mass contained maggots which were trying to dig into the stained grout.

In a frenzy she knocked over the half-glass of Cutty Sark. The whiskey flooded the maggots, causing them to bob and weave violently. Her stomach heaved as she ran to the sink. More of the larvae splattered the yellowed porcelain. Beverly fought for control.

When the wave of nausea had subsided, she ran for the kitchen door that led out to the garden. *I need medical help now, not tomorrow.* She tripped down the back stairs and landed on some flagstones that had been arbitrarily laid out. Convulsive coughing brought the writhing insects up into her mouth. The maggots bubbled out between her lips, coaxing their way down her chin or falling to the earth, where they swiftly buried themselves. Beverly spat out saliva and larvae for several seconds until she could vaguely feel one lone survivor poking around under her tongue. Using an index finger, she scooped the vermin out and smeared its body against a flagstone. She looked at her hand and cringed. She hesitated before wiping her finger across the front of her shirt. Gasping for air, she tried to calm herself.

Slowly she climbed to her knees and stood unsteadily. Night had already embraced the wood. But she had to get help. If she suffered from internal as well as external tissue necrosis, she couldn't have long to live. Perhaps only a few hours.

The dirt path led her down to the river. Confused, she tried to remember in which direction the town lay. The water was peaceful and black. A quarter-moon cast a faint glow across the river and the land.

Unable to stand any longer, Beverly sat on a small boulder, the river side of which had been covered with moss. She was neither cold nor warm. Faintly her body ached, but not as much as it should, given its condition. She sat silent, still, attempting to recapture her former acumen and puzzle out her next move. She felt as if the still night were revolving around her.

She shivered, but not from cold. When she looked down at her body, she grimaced to see the stinking blotched flesh.

Yes, Beverly now knew the direction to town, but she did not think she could complete the trip. She didn't want to become carrion for the animals. No one would be out walking in the dark or, for that matter, rowing on the river. If she could survive until dawn, she could attempt the trip in daylight. Beverly panted, trying to replace the oxygen that her body seemed to use so poorly now.

Patiently, Death waited, soundlessly, painlessly offering her the peace of oblivion. However, she didn't want the gift. How had she managed to live this long in her condition? she wondered. And might she not last until dawn? She looked back in the direction of the house, which promised protection against the night's predators.

Chapter 4
The Hiker

Megan packed up camp immediately after breakfast. She hated to travel alone, but her roommate, Hester, had wimped out three days before, taking a bus to the nearest airport to catch a flight back home. "None of this roughing it for me" were her parting words as the driver loaded her backpack.

Megan refused to give up. She wanted to cross the state on foot and would do it. However, she might have to do it half asleep since, alone in the woods, she found it almost impossible to sleep through the night. Occasionally she would doze, then find herself sitting bolt upright when an animal cried out or the wind rustled the leaves too loudly. She was definitely not the pioneer type, having been raised in large cities throughout the country. Ah! The life of an Army brat.

Once her sleeping bag was rolled up, she met her greatest challenge head on—namely, trying to fit it back inside the sack. While doing this, Megan broke her last surviving fingernail. *Looked stupid anyway,* she consoled herself.

To a 22 year-old straight out of college, traveling seemed like the best prospect in a depressed economy. Didn't cost very much to sleep on the ground, and when she felt a bit gamey she would find herself a motel with a real shower instead of the chilly stream water she had been dabbing on her face. She was experiencing life in the raw. Hester couldn't appreciate the wonders of nature.

A long-legged spider crawled out of the sleeping bag sack. Megan dropped the sack and let out a tiny, disgusted squeal. It must have been in the sack, not her bedroll, she kept telling herself over and over again as she waited for the spider to leap from sack to ground. When it became apparent that the spider was probably as frozen from fear as she was, Megan lifted a branch and with a jerking motion slid the branch across the sack, sweeping the spider to the ground. She hoped that was what had happened, but she couldn't be sure since she couldn't find the spider.

She lifted the sack and held it at arm's length, slowly turning it to inspect for intruders. It ap-

peared that only a few leaves and twigs hugged
the bright orange material. She dusted the sack
off and put it with the rest of her equipment,
then loaded the whole bundle on her back.

Megan pulled a small compass out of her
jeans pocket, checked the sun, returned the
compass to its close quarters, and resumed her
march down the path she had been following
the day before. Her hiking boots crushed the
debris on the trail. She stumbled over a rock
that was partly raised from the soil and landed
hard on her right knee, skinning the palms of
both her hands.

"Grrrrww . . ." she growled, angry and hurt.

When she looked down at her right leg, she
saw that her worn jeans had split open at the
knee, revealing a not-very-deep cut. She sat on
the dirt-packed trail, wondering whether the
wound was worth pulling her backpack apart
to find the first-aid kit. She used spit to clean
away most of the dirt from the cut. There was
some blood, but not enough to panic over.

Megan slipped off the backpack and went digging for bandages. By the time she found gauze
and tape, the wound had crusted over. She
smeared antiseptic across her knee, just in case,
and covered it with the bandage. After repack-
ing, she started to stand.

"Ow . . . ow . . . ow . . . ow," she whispered as
the skin on her wounded knee began to stretch.
Once she was standing, Megan lifted the backpack and slid each arm into the straps, then
continued down the trail, limping.

By noon she was walking with less of a limp; however, her stomach was complaining audibly. Just ahead she caught a glimpse of a watery reflection. She could stop at the lake, stream, or whatever, have lunch, then bathe in the water. Perfect, she thought.

It wasn't a stream, Megan realized as she approached the wide river. Walking along the water's edge, she looked for a good place to stop and perhaps catch some fish. Inside the backpack were fishing line and flies. Megan remembered fishing with her father. He always baited the hook; she never had to touch the squiggly worm at the end of the line. If either caught a fish that they wouldn't want to eat, Dad would gently remove the hook and toss the panting fish back into the water. Up until age twelve, she had loved those expeditions; then her mind had turned to boys, and Dad's favorite hobby had taken a backseat.

Up ahead Megan spotted a rowboat. She could tell it had recently been taken out of the water, since the underside, which was lying upward, was shimmering in the strong midday sun. Megan approached slowly, for she had not yet met any of the locals and didn't know how they would react to trespassing.

Eventually a slim smokestack appeared through the trees. Pushing away some of the bushes, Megan left the trail and headed toward a small house that was barely visible. Finally she could see several wicker chairs arranged in a semicircle around a glass-topped table on the porch of the house. The jalousies were closed against the hot sun.

Gosh, it would be great to sit down to a home-cooked meal, she thought. *What's the worst they can do? Shoot me?* Megan bravely proceeded up toward the house, the gravel crunching under her steps.

As she approached the house, her senses were flooded by the smell of hyacinths. Megan took a deep breath, enjoying the sweetness, and walked around to the back of the house to see the garden. As she pushed open the waist-high gate, Megan was awed by the variety of flowers. There were roses of various colors and shades. There were carnations and daisies, both yellow and white, but the prevailing odor in the air was from the hyacinths. Megan walked to a big elm that sheltered a whitewashed garden swing.

She was about to sit when she heard a door slam. Swiftly she turned to see French doors, the filmy curtains on the inside rustling with a life she could not make out.

"Hi, I didn't mean to intrude, but . . ." What excuse could she give? She wondered whether she should quietly retreat from the garden. Suddenly the outline of a body slammed into the curtains and the French doors. The doors gave a little with the force but remained closed. Abruptly the figure withdrew and the doors gave up their sag and the curtains fluttered to a free-hanging standstill.

Megan scratched her head. Maybe it hadn't been a good idea to come up to the house.

She strode toward the gate. At first it seemed to stick, but with a firm nudge from her good knee the gate flew open. While making a face toward the French doors, Megan closed the gate and pivoted around to walk back to the river, occasionally turning to look at the house. It was freshly painted a pale yellow, with antique white on the trim and the porch. Ivy crept up the stairs while flowering bushes surrounded the front of the house. It would be inviting except for its occupant.

As she drew closer to the river, she could see one of the jalousies move slightly. Whoever it was must have decided to watch, perhaps to make sure the intruder moved on. Megan peered back as if she could see through the obstruction. Suddenly she toppled over the rowboat, injuring her cut knee once again.

"Damn," she squealed. "Why must I be so clumsy?"

Megan clasped both her hands over her reinjured knee and held her breath for a few seconds, waiting for the pain to subside. Finally she released the knee and slowly straightened her leg. The gauze was soaked red. She groaned. Now she would have to change the bandage.

Megan threw off her backpack and searched for the first-aid kit again.

"You'd think I'd learn. Do I pack it toward the top so it's easily accessible? No. I just throw it in anywhere it fits. Megan, you have to put some order in your life if you expect to survive this trip," she loudly scolded. The sound of her own voice gave her courage.

"Can I help you, Megan?"

She looked up to see an attractive older man, not very tall, perhaps five feet six or seven, but his shoulders were broad and he had a confident expression and body language.

"Sorry. Is this your boat?" Megan looked over at the toppled rowboat.

"Yes, and I should say I'm sorry for leaving it where it could be tripped over. However, not many people come this way."

"I know. I've spent the past few days communing with nature ever since Hester left me."

"Hester?" The man looked around.

"She went home. Didn't take to roughing it."

The man turned his gaze back down to Megan and nodded. He seemed to be memorizing what he saw.

"Your house?" she asked, pointing behind him.

He nodded.

"I'm sorry if I disturbed you up there. I wanted to see the garden. The smell of the hyacinths was so strong."

His eyes darkened and the blue pigment turned to an inky hue that froze her. His mouth tightened, the hint of tiny lines creasing the outline of his lips.

Megan's head swiveled toward her backpack.

"Like I said, I'm sorry. I just want to take care of my knee, and then I'm gone."

The man squatted down, and his eyes softened at the sight of the bloodstained gauze. He reached across the distance between them and touched her knee. She winced at his heavy touch. He pulled his hand back.

"You shouldn't be walking on that knee. Why not come back to my place? You'll be able to bathe." Megan thought his nose twitched when he said it. "Also, I have some fresh bandages."

"Bandages I have," she said, whipping out another slab of gauze. However, the bathtub sounded inviting. Megan looked up toward the house. Was it safe to bathe in a stranger's home?

"Thank you, but I'll be all right as soon as I change this."

She scrunched up her face in preparation for pulling off the wet gauze.

"If you do it quickly, it won't hurt so much."

Megan looked into the man's eyes. They had transformed into a light, reflective blue softened by a hint of a smile dancing in his pupils.

"I know." With shoulders drawn up to her ears, she ripped the gauze strip away from the wound. Her whole body relaxed.

"You should really clean that cut," the man said.

Megan looked at him, then at the house. If he had meant any harm, he probably would have done something when she had been in the garden. Remembering the force that had hit the French doors, she turned to the stranger and asked, "Do you live alone? I mean, do you have a wife, kids?"

The man took a deep breath, then moved from a squatting position to sit on the damp grass. She was going to warn him about staining his linen trousers, but it was too late. He crossed his legs in front of him.

"I live alone. Never been blessed with a wife or a daughter like you, Megan." He smiled, and his lush lips invited exploration.

She decided it was better to smear some more of the antiseptic on her knee and cover it with fresh gauze than to soak in his bathtub. Her knee tingled as she applied the brown tincture. She pressed the gauze softly down onto the wound and watched the brown from the ointment spread out under the cloth's edges.

Megan wavered as she started to stand. He quickly stood next to her, offering his hand. It was crusted with scabs. She placed her small, soft hand in his, sensing his strength and the hardness of his life.

"I don't believe you'll make it much farther along the river on foot."

"Actually, I was going to stop here for lunch, but I got curious and . . ." Megan shrugged.

"Come back with me and at least rest for a few hours. I'll even feed you," he offered with a laugh.

Her stomach, which had been silent during

her inspection of the garden, started to growl again.

"Haven't eaten in a while, have you?"

Megan shook her head. She watched him laugh as he pulled her closer. One of her hands was in his; the other rested on the cool cotton of his shirt.

"Why don't you sit in the shade while I put the boat in the water?"

"Boat?"

"Yes. You will come back to my place." It wasn't a question or merely a statement. It was a command.

"But don't you live up there?" she asked, pointing at the yellow house with the white trim.

"No!" His voice softened as he explained, "That house I rent out. It's empty now because I have some work I have to do on it. My place is not far from here. You'll enjoy it on the river. It's cooler than being earthbound." He led her to the shade of a tree, then went to right his rowboat and set it adrift in the water.

Megan looked back at the house and thought she saw a jalousie move, but decided it was a trick of the sunlight.

Chapter 5
The Hyacinths

Beverly's hand slid across the window slats, sealing herself in and the world out. She had watched the young girl step into Carl's rowboat, had watched him push off, then jump into the boat and row out of sight.

Her decaying body leaned against the frame of the window, resting from its own heaviness. She wondered why Carl had returned that day. It was almost as if he needed to know that she was still here. Where could she have gone? Her body was no longer mobile enough to travel, and the nearest town was miles away.

Beverly stood as straight as she could, but it was becoming difficult. Her spine seemed to waver. Vertebrae seemed to be planted in sludge in which they settled deeper and deeper with time. There was little pain except for the constant nibbling in her gut and the bouts of asphyxiation. Every other breath was deep; if she failed to take the deep breath, she would feel light-headed. She had lost consciousness several times since yesterday.

Naked, she walked toward her bedroom. Beverly had eliminated all clothing when she found that anything binding her skin made deep crevices, which loosened the underlying flesh, causing the surface skin to slough off in sheets. She didn't know why, but she was determined to last as long as possible.

Once inside the bedroom, Beverly moved to the French doors. Carl had stood there earlier, talking about destroying the hyacinths she had planted. She wasn't sure whether he had been talking to her or himself, since his back had been turned toward her. Beverly hadn't seen the girl until he had slammed the doors shut. When she tried to signal the girl, he had dragged Beverly across the room and flung her against the wall in the hallway. Repentant, he had tried to touch her face. She had pulled away, wishing she could scream, but her parched throat could only utter whispers now.

As she opened the French doors, Beverly's lips smiled, cracking the skin and allowing tiny rivulets of blood to trickle down her mouth. The bell-shaped flowers stood a foot tall before her, some white, some blue, but the majority were a deep purple-blue. She had planted them in the fall, a day or two after signing the lease for the house. Beverly panted, trying to take in the scent of her favorite flowers. It was becoming harder to catch their odor. Finally, when their sweetness was caught within her body, she relaxed, savoring the morsel allowed her.

Beverly walked into the garden but stopped when the sun hit her disintegrating flesh. She was afire. The pain singed her soul, and she cried out inaudibly. Her mouth shaped in an O, she turned her face up to the sun, which seared her eyes shut. Beverly threw herself onto the bedroom floor. Splayed across the wooden planks, she wept.

Impulsively, Beverly grabbed the down comforter off the bed and wrapped herself entirely in its quilted folds. Again she attempted to step out into the sun, but the blazing rays reached through the thick coverlet to singe her flesh, forcing her to retreat back into her bedroom.

Her only protection against the sun was the shelter of the house. Nausea flooded through her as she realized the impossibility of walking to town by day. *Like the mythical vampire, I am neither living nor dead.* Carl hadn't lied.

No one would come for her except Carl, when he thought nothing but bones were left. Her friends knew that she had gone into seclusion to complete her new book. They hadn't even asked her destination, knowing how she liked to work in solitude. Her brother was out of the country and wouldn't think about her again until the holidays rolled around.

Initially, the concept of Carl's spell had seemed ludicrous to her. But her flesh still steamed from the sun's touch and vermin still spewed from orifices. Yet she hadn't died. Carl hadn't lied. There was no way she could obtain medical help. The sun's scorching burn kept her housebound. Traveling by night, she would either get lost or not make it to town before dawn. Her ash and bone would scatter in a summer breeze before she could ask for help. And Carl would have won. The young girl would be her replacement. Instinct told her to hold tight and wait. Perhaps survival was impossible; however, revenge might come to her through Carl himself.

Beverly reached up to touch her tears and felt the sockets of her eyes bulging out beyond the frame of her face. Lord, what did she look like? All the mirrors must be destroyed. She could not bear to watch this transformation from life to death. Is growing old anything like this? Perhaps she should think of it as accelerated aging, but that was no solace for a 35 year-old woman.

Chapter 6
What Smell?

Carl watched Megan as he rowed. She was a pretty girl, a bit too thin, yet he could see the swell of her breasts beneath the denim shirt. Her red hair, curling around her face, was maturing from bright orange into a softer hue. The few freckles scattered across the bridge of her nose detracted only because they made her look childlike. Otherwise, her features were even, cheekbones high, and there was a definite shape to her pouty lips. Heart-shaped, he supposed some would call it. Overall, he decided she was a find.

"The water feels so fresh and cool."

He noticed her right hand slipping through the water, leaving a trail that quickly dissolved.

"So you started out with your friend Hester.

You think she may attempt to join up with you again?"

"Are you kidding? No way. She wouldn't know where to look for me anyhow. We didn't have a very well-laid-out plan to begin with, so Hester wouldn't be able to find me even if she wanted to. No, I'll see her again when I return home in another month and a half."

Carl nodded and smiled.

"How's your knee?"

Megan looked down at the bandaged knee peeking out from her shredded jeans. She winced when she tried to extend the leg a little. He knew the wound was stiffening up. By the time they reached land, she would hardly be able to walk.

"Okay, I guess."

He noted the frown on her face. Twenty, maybe twenty-one, he thought. He liked the frown; it made her look older.

"Have you been living in the area a long time?"

"Past few years. Your parents must be worried about you traveling alone."

"Dad died when I was fifteen, and I don't speak to Mom. I have no siblings, so who's to worry?"

Carl tried to look compassionate, but found it hard to conceal the inner joy he felt.

"It's sad when a parent and child don't communicate."

"It's sad when one has a mother who wants to be as young as you are." Megan paused. "Things changed after Dad died. For a while, neither my mother nor I knew what to do. We managed to keep our house, and there was a generous insurance policy and widow's pension, but then Mom started dating . . . well . . . boys. They were all just a few years older than me. It was dreadful never knowing when my own mother might try to steal my boyfriend. She never did, but a lot of Dad's cash went toward seducing her young bucks. Lucky I had a trust fund for college. I was able to live away from home, and I haven't spoken to my mom since the day I loaded up my old car and headed to school."

"When will you be graduating?"

"I did this past January. Been kind of kicking around ever since. I had waitress jobs, salesclerk, even had a bit part in a play, although it paid hardly anything. I'm an anthropology major—not much call for people like us."

Carl felt the muscles in his arms swell as he rowed. He was becoming stronger every minute. He hoped Beverly would last awhile, because he was enjoying Megan's company.

"You know, I've traveled considerably, Megan, and you may want to examine some of my books and journals. I've visited several tribes in the Amazon basin." Carl made a mental note to conceal the last journal under the back porch of his house.

Megan replied with some enthusiasm, but Carl was able to see that she didn't plan on staying around long. He would have to change her mind.

When they got close to land, Carl jumped out into the water to drag the boat up on the soil. Megan tried to stand, but instead let out a soft squeal.

"Stay seated. I'll help you in a moment."

He felt as if he were bursting with strength as he easily pulled the boat and its occupant onto the landing.

Once the boat was secure, he turned to Megan. He saw the surprise on her face when he picked her up.

"I can walk, really. It's just a little stiff."

Carl ignored her and continued up the path. Midway to the house, he was assaulted by the scent of hyacinths. His stomach roiled under the sweet odor. His arms sagged a bit and he could feel Megan's arms tighten around his neck. Carl forced the strength back into his limbs and walked past the grave.

Inside the house, Carl went straight to his bedroom and placed Megan atop the chenille coverlet. He felt the wetness of her hands as they slipped from his neck, and he smelled her fear, which was an improvement over the damn hyacinths.

"I noticed a couch in the living room. I'd prefer that, if you don't mind." She was going to try to stare him down on this. Her brown eyes looked like black dots, with bursts of fire circling them.

"Relax, Megan. There's an adjoining bathroom. I thought I would run a bath for you. If you don't mind my saying so, you are a little ripe." Actually, he liked her odor. It was a mingling of fear, curiosity, and youthful sensuality.

As Carl walked into the bathroom, the mirror facing him reflected the image of Megan on the bed. He saw her sniff under an armpit and bend her head forward for a general whiff of her body. Carl chuckled while turning on the water taps.

When he returned to the bedroom, Megan extended her hand and said, "I'm Megan."

"I'm sorry, Megan. Carl." He gently took her hand in both of his, then brought it up to his lips. Megan swiftly retrieved her hand. "The bath is ready. Can I help you?" he said while unlacing her hiking boots.

"Carl, I appreciate the bath, but I've been tying and untying my laces since I was two."

"A prodigy."

"No, just independent."

Carl spread his arms wide, then gestured toward the bathroom.

"How about some help in walking to the bathroom?"

Megan slid her legs across the coverlet and dropped each leg down the side of the bed, remembering to keep her right leg straight. When she stood, she reached out for Carl's support.

He walked her to the bathroom and waited there until she closed the door in his face. Carl blew out some air. He decided to wait outside the house, since there was no lock on the bathroom door and the temptation was too great.

Once on the redwood deck, Carl remembered Megan's backpack and began to walk down the path toward his boat, but midway he was again assailed by the hyacinths. He left the path. When he reached the grave, he noticed that even the petunias were dead now. Nothing flowered on or around the grave. Yet there was the odor of the hyacinths.

"Witch," he muttered. Many times he had buried images that prolonged his life, but never had he experienced such an olfactory hallucination before. Maybe he loved Beverly more than he recognized. He sat by the grave and thought about digging the coffin up. What would he find? A shroud of hyacinths?

Carl smoothed over the soil with his hand. He knew Beverly had seen him leave with Megan. Would she be jealous? When he had buried the drawing, he had promised himself that he would make Beverly as comfortable as possible while she was dying, but now Megan was here.

"Sorry, Beverly." He patted the grave. He thought the soil trembled under his hand. Carl arose and buried his hands deep inside his trousers pockets. Before returning to the house, he retrieved Megan's backpack from the boat. On his way back, he planned the meal that he and Megan would share.

He moved through the threshold of the front door, dropped the pack on the living-room floor, then turned left into the kitchen while humming.

"Back already?"

Carl saw Megan seated at the kitchen table, munching some Edam cheese. She was wearing only his navy terry robe. The porcelain skin of her long legs showed through the front opening. She had tied the belt loosely, so the top slid a bit off her shoulder. He could tell that she had recognized his lecherous leer, because she immediately readjusted the garment.

"I borrowed your robe. My clothes were a bit 'ripe,' too, so I also washed them in the tub and hung them over some rocks in the backyard. In this heat, they should dry quickly."

"Too quickly," he muttered.

"What?"

"How about I make us a real meal while you're nibbling on that cheese?" He saw her eyes brighten. The brown irises were a warmer, more earthy shade than before, and the fire had cooled into promising embers.

It was impossible for him to avoid. He touched her shoulder.

"Mmmmm. I love that smell," she said.

"What smell?"

"Hyacinths."

Carl briskly pulled away his hand. He hurried to the sink, turned on the faucets, and scrubbed his hands with soap.

Chapter 7
A Loaf of Bread, a Jug of Wine . . .

Megan watched Carl scrub his hands. She thought that he would rub them raw if she didn't do something to stop him. As she rose from her chair, she popped another slice of cheese into her mouth. This man intrigued her. Kind of sexy for an old guy, she pondered. *Bite your tongue*, Megan chastised herself. Certainly he didn't consider himself old. Through the window, sunlight flashed into her eyes as she approached Carl.

There was blood on his hands. He had broken open several calluses.

"Do you always scrub down like a doctor before cooking a meal?"

Carl turned to Megan, looked at her, then at

his hands. A few seconds of silence passed before he laughed.

"Hand me the towel over there, Megan."

She glanced across the kitchen in the direction he had pointed. As she went for the towel, she heard the water stop.

"So what are we having to eat?"

Megan and Carl worked together in the kitchen, scraping vegetables, trimming meat, and baking bread. By the time they were finished, the kitchen was a mess, but Megan found the food delicious. Carl poured several glasses of wine for Megan as she drank, munched, and giggled. She was used to having pizza and beer on Friday nights at college, but the heady, mellow feel of the wine was new.

"I feel kind of warm and safe right here." She pointed to the middle of her abdomen. It was twilight, and she recalled the foreboding she had felt the previous day at that time. "I dreaded being alone last night in the woods. All sorts of weird ideas went through my head. Newspaper accounts of young girls found dead in the country and supernatural tales of demons preying on innocent female victims."

"Why are you doing it, then?"

"Because I started out to do it, and I'll finish it."

"I hope at least you'll accept my hospitality for tonight."

Megan was relieved, but also wary of this seductive man. He wasn't the kind of handsome that girls tittered over, yet there was something charismatic and bold. She had been so entranced in studying him that her body jolted when she noticed he was returning the stare. Megan gulped down some wine, trying to think of a cool reply that would also allow her to stay the night without any commitment to more than sleeping under his roof.

"You can have my bed. I'll sleep on the couch in the living room," he said, as if reading her mind.

"There's my bedroll."

"The couch would be more comfortable for me."

"No, I meant I can sleep on the bedroll in the living room. I don't want to take the bed away from you."

"Okay."

Megan was disappointed. The bed had felt soft that afternoon, especially after she had slept on the ground the past several nights.

"Something wrong, Megan?"

Everyone told her that her face gave her away. They said it was the pout of her lower lip that signaled her black moods.

"No," she said, bringing her napkin up to press against her mouth.

When Carl stood, Megan started piling the dishes.

"Leave them and come into the living room with me."

Megan guessed that piling the dishes was easier for her than the task of standing. She was lightheaded. The alcohol also anesthetized the knee wound, she realized as she stretched the injured leg. Was this the buzz the others at the dorm had talked about? Her limit had always been one beer and five slices of pizza; it seemed she enjoyed eating more than imbibing. Tonight had been different. She had cleaned her plate; still, she hadn't eaten more than her share. However, the wine bottle was empty, and Carl had only been sipping from his glass.

"Ummm. Maybe we could take a walk?"

Carl looked at her closely.

"Not used to drinking?"

"Just beer. A little air might help, and perhaps some assistance in standing," she said while making an effort to rise.

"Bed might be a better place for you," he said, approaching her.

"No! I don't want to go to sleep. I'm enjoying your company too much."

Megan watched a smile broaden Carl's wide features.

"Give me your hands, Megan."

She did. With her palms touching his, Megan staggered to the soles of her bare feet. It was the first time she noticed that the two of them were almost the same height. She had known he wasn't very tall, yet hadn't considered the fact that they were almost equals in any aspect.

He pulled her close to him, leaning his face close to hers, and spoke. "You smell irresistible."

Her palms started to sweat.

"Must be your own soap."

"There's no perfume in the soap I make, but there is a sensual fragrance to you."

Time to leave, she thought, yet she allowed him to breathe softly upon her ear.

"I feel dizzy. Too much wine. I need some air, please."

She felt his sigh against her earlobe. Megan pulled back her hands and tried to wobble through the kitchen threshold on her own.

"Here, take my arm," he called, swiftly moving to intercept her at the doorway.

Megan smiled at him, then clung to the sleeve of his cotton shirt while trying to ignore the hot flesh beneath it.

Carl and Megan walked out onto a redwood deck and down several stairs until Megan could feel the earth beneath her. She listened to her feet slap against the dirt with an unsteady rhythm. Carl was silent. Megan glanced at him to judge his mood, but it was too dark to obtain a clear view of his features. Perhaps she should test the waters to see how annoyed he might be. She tried to conjure up an innocuous question that would not imply anything in particular. As her mind raced through the possibilities, she lost awareness of her surroundings until the sweet smell of hyacinths exploded her senses. *That's it*, she thought.

"Your hyacinths smell lovely."

Carl's arm stiffened, and he tried to move her

forward when she stopped to luxuriate in the fragrance.

"Come, Megan."

Megan let go of his arm and turned in the direction of the aroma.

"You've planted them over there, haven't you?" She started to move off the path. Carl lifted her off her feet and carried her back to the house.

He was angry; she could feel the tension spread across his shoulders into his arms, hard fingers digging into her thigh where the robe had parted.

"I'm sorry," she whispered like a repentant child. She had meant to reduce the strain between them; instead, it had been increased.

Carl's shoes hit the steps, climbing with determination. He crossed the deck and entered the house, but didn't release her until they were in the bedroom, where he literally dropped her onto the coverlet. She had liked it better that afternoon, when she had been deposited with obvious affection.

"You will sleep here tonight."

"But it's still early. I'd like to see the garden," she protested, rebellion automatically countering his command.

Carl shook his head.

"When you are able to walk on your own without assistance, then you can explore my property." Carl started for the door, then halted to turn toward Megan. "By the way, there is no garden." He left with a slam of the door.

No garden? she thought. Maybe he meant a planned garden. Perhaps someone else had planted the hyacinths, and now they grew wild. That must be it.

Megan pulled the coverlet down on the opposite side of the bed, then scooted her rear onto the sheet so that she could pull down the other side. *Mmmmm, sheets*, she thought. Clean sheets. Megan plumped the two pillows on the bed and got under the top sheet. Was it safe to sleep naked? she wondered as she touched the belt of the robe. She laughed at herself.

"If he was going to rape you, Megan, he would have already done it." She brushed a hand across her mouth, sealing her lips. After all, she didn't want to give him any ideas.

Her hands unknotted the belt. Slowly she slipped out of the robe. She tried to throw it onto a chair near the window, but it landed instead on a small Persian rug. She cursed.

Could she pick the robe up? she wondered. She should, she knew. Not very polite to fling other people's clothing on the floor. Mother didn't think it polite when Megan threw her own clothes on the floor, but that was just a minor dispute between the two women.

Megan slipped to the edge of the bed and dangled her legs off the side. Taking a deep breath, she stood and shut her eyes as the room seemed to spin around her. When she opened her eyes, she fixed her sight on the robe and walked.

Bending down to pick the robe up was an additional problem, which Megan solved by using her foot to slowly bring the garment up to her hand. Her body wavered on one foot for a few seconds as her tongue protruded out and to the side of her mouth, as if assisting in the balancing act. Once she felt the nubby material in her hand, she dropped her foot back down onto the rug. Gingerly, she reached out to place the robe on the wicker chair in front of her. Ordeal completed, Megan moved to the window to the right of the chair. It was shut tight. She shook her head. A wonder he didn't suffocate in this room, she thought. Megan pulled up the window frame and smiled as the breeze swept the room with the essence of hyacinths.

Chapter 8
No Sense Denying the Hyacinths

In the study Carl sat scrunched down in his chair, legs spread wide across the worn Oriental rug. His arms lay heavily on the armrests. His body was still except for the rise and fall of his chest.

He hadn't expected to sleep on the couch that night, but then, he hadn't expected Megan to sleep there, either.

Carl sat up and slid open the bottom drawer of his desk. He pulled out a sketch pad and charcoal pencil. After thumbing through a few rough drafts of Beverly, he found a blank page. He closed his eyes and visualized Megan, how the red curls dipped down on her forehead, the smooth surface of her skin, the almond shape of her eyes, lids heavy with long lashes lifting them romantically halfway. Her eyes always looked as if they were hiding a secret.

Carl's own lids opened slowly. He stared at the page. He'd need more time. It was crucial that he see more of the frame of her body. If he could get her to stay a few more days, he would have no trouble in examining her body in detail. Carl always had been lucky when it came to women.

A door squeaked. Carl got up and went into the hallway, catching Megan creeping out of the bedroom, clutching the navy robe around her. Under the dim hall light, Carl was stunned by the contrast between her pale legs and the dark material draping her body, a body he lusted after and envied for its obvious health.

"How's the knee?" he asked, trying to pinpoint some flaw.

Megan jumped.

"Oh! I didn't expect to see you."

"It's my home."

"Yes, but I didn't want to bother you."

Carl reminded himself that he wanted two things from this girl: sex and life.

"I shouldn't have been so abrupt with you before. I was angry with myself for giving you too much to drink. Are you feeling better?"

Megan nodded. "Just thirsty."

He smiled, wondering whether the night could be salvaged.

"Go back to bed. I'll bring some water."

He could see that she was ready to refuse, but then her throat moved as though she were swallowing her pride.

"Okay," she said in a juvenile manner.

Off she went to bed, as Carl flipped off the wall switch for the light in his study. He hoped he wouldn't be returning to that room tonight.

In the kitchen Carl let the faucet run for a few seconds before filling a glass. She was vulnerable. He had seen her stare at him with the sexual curiosity of a novice. Actually she had gawked, relying on the heaviness of her lids to hide the passion simmering beyond the stares. He must be sure to touch her hand as he passed her the water. Perhaps he could chance sitting on the bed; she was too insecure to reprimand him. A few soft touches, a fluffing of the pillow below her head . . .

Carl put the glass on the counter and rubbed his chin. This was the first time he had ever planned out his pursuit. It had always been natural for him. It was different this time; there was desperation inside of him. Beverly was different from the prior women; she haunted him. He would have to dispose of her sooner than the others. He couldn't trust her to run out the journey to the end. While she still had a spark of life, he would douse her with kerosene, burn her down to ash and bone, then put the remains in a weighted sack and carry them down to the river.

He wished there were some flowers nearby

that he could bring Megan in order to topple the barrier between them, but he'd have to forage through his backyard for wildflowers. It was too dark to consider that option.

Carl took a sip of the water himself. Too warm, he thought, and decided to add an ice cube. On the way to the refrigerator, he passed the table on which the dirty dishes were piled. He noticed an ant crawling across one of the plates, exploring, popping in and out of unseen mazes in its haste to find food. Carl pressed his thumb down on the ant; then he wiped the finger on a napkin, leaving an unrecognizable smear. He threw the paper napkin into the garbage pail.

After retrieving some ice from the freezer and plopping it into the glass, Carl made his way to his own bedroom door, knocking before entering. Without waiting for her reply, Carl opened the door and stepped into the room.

His hand shook, spilling some water onto the floor. The sweet hyacinth fragrance so permeated the room that he could feel his gorge rise into his throat. After swallowing several times, he realized that Megan had taken the glass and was asking if he was all right. Turning to her, he saw the open window behind her and shoved her aside as he raced to it. Carl grabbed the top of the frame and pushed down, but it was stuck.

"You bitch!" he yelled. Finally the window gave under the weight of his palms. The glass shook as the frame slammed down on the sill.

From behind him he could hear Megan repeating the words "I'm sorry." He wanted to shut her up and toss the meddlesome girl out of his home, but only she could free him from that wretched woman.

Unable to think clearly in the midst of the swirling fragrance, Carl left the room and made sure he closed the door softly. Megan had been shocked enough for one evening.

Once in the hallway, Carl was able to evaluate the situation. If he didn't calm Megan down, she might leave during the night. He couldn't allow that. He would never allow her to leave until he had drawn her.

"Megan," he called.

She opened the door. One of her hands held the doorknob; the other still clutched the water glass.

"Come into the living room and let me explain." He didn't know how to make her understand his behavior, but he had to revive her interest and trust in him.

"Maybe it would be best if we slept before we talked."

"No, Megan. I don't want you to be frightened." He looked into her eyes. "Will you be able to sleep tonight after what happened in there?"

She shrugged her shoulders. He could tell that she didn't want to deal with the problem, perhaps was planning her getaway.

"Please, Megan. I've been alone here for a long time. I was numb until you came. I've been able to talk and laugh with you tonight. Don't take that away from me. At least, let me explain my . . ." he paused, "eccentricities."

"You were angry."

"Not with you."

"Who is the 'bitch,' then?"

Carl realized he should have used the plural of that word, but was relieved he hadn't.

"The hyacinth smell reminds me of an old love, who left for someone else."

"She planted the flowers?"

There was no sense denying the hyacinths now. Let her look for the ghostly plants. Carl nodded.

He watched Megan's eyes grow soft, her lips part, and he could see that one of her front teeth was slightly crooked. He made special note of that.

"You know, instead of this water, I'd like some juice. I noticed you had some oranges on the kitchen counter. Why don't we squeeze some and maybe have a second helping of tonight's dessert?"

She was appeased so much that she took his hand as they walked into the kitchen.

Small hands, he thought, slender. The veins protruded more on the right hand than the left, the knuckles bulged a little, the nails were ragged . . .

Chapter 9
Look at Me!

The attentive round eyes glowed in her direction. They observed her while the small nose twitched the whiskers underneath. Slowly the upper flap of its mouth eased back, revealing sharp teeth between which Beverly could see the saliva glisten.

"You can almost taste me," she whispered.

The rodent rested on its haunches, the six-inch tail curled beside its body. It smelled the rotting flesh but had seen Beverly move, so it was being cautious. Ten feet between them, the air dripped with the scent of carrion.

Beverly waited a few more seconds until she saw the rat's back legs tense, ready for the jump. Before the rat could pounce, Beverly, with all the force left to her, flung a crystal vase at the rat. The rodent scurried through the open

French doors and into the garden. Six feet from the house, the rat stopped and turned to stare at Beverly briefly before rushing into the bushes. It would be back; how much longer could she exist?

Beverly walked toward the French doors, not feeling the glass underfoot as it sliced open the soles of her feet. She hated to close the doors, since her sense of smell seemed to be fading and the only consolation she had was the garden, especially the hyacinths. However, for her own safety, she had to close the doors at night. She thought about how disappointed the rat must be to see the doors slam shut against it. Beverly pulled aside the curtain on the chance that she might see the rodent again under the moonlight. Nothing rustled the garden except a thin breeze, which hardly touched anything.

This was the first time she had confronted the creature in her bedroom. Normally, the rats had stayed in the bushes, watching. With time, they were becoming brave. At least one had. A scout for the rest, she speculated.

Beverly paced the house, not knowing what to look for or do, but wanting to reinforce in her mind that she was alive. There was no longer any need for sleep. She was never tired but always languid. Her motions were limited by decay and the fear that more of her would vanish from her bones with any sudden movement. The flesh was so worn away on her forearms that she could see the veins winding down her naked elbow joint to the folds of flesh hanging about her wrist.

She stopped in front of her bathroom mirror. She had been unwilling to destroy the looking glass that enabled her to measure her time in the world. The top of the skull was bare now, the forehead pronounced, the eye sockets settled deep in her face. The cartilage on the bridge of her nose was squishy to the touch and was spread across the upper part of her cheeks. The lips were a pale purple. The chin was starting to blacken.

She spread the palm of her hand across the mirror and softly rubbed her reflection, leaving a filmy scum of cells to mar the glass. Suddenly she could see Carl's features, rough, uneven, yet handsome, resting against her pillow. His eyes were shut against her face.

"Look at me!" she screamed in the highest whisper her rancid throat would allow, but his face seemed to turn away from her into the softness of the pillow.

"Damn you! Look at me! Look at what you did!"

Her heavy sobs choked off her breath, and she panicked. Panting for air, she threw open the bathroom window. The buttery hue of the moon crossed her countenance, penetrating the threads of skin on her lower jaw, revealing the meaty rawness of what was underneath.

Beverly breathed in the dew of the night, clearing her vision and allowing her lungs to tuck into their decaying sacs some precious oxygen. Without warning, an animal jumped down upon her naked head, scratching the blackening skin into open pockets. With both her hands, Beverly flung the rodent against one of the tiled bathroom walls. Dazed, the animal quivered as Beverly reached for its tail. She smashed its head against the porcelain tub until its brains smeared a path on the whiteness of the tub's surface. Then her hands went limp, letting the rat fall to the floor.

A high-pitched gurgle ushered forth from Beverly's throat as she backed out of the bathroom. She wondered where the violence in her came from. Was it always there? Or did it come from Carl? Had she taken on his indifference to the lives of others?

No, she knew it was her instincts keeping her alive, keeping her prepared, although she did not know for what.

Chapter 10
Beauty Mark Under
Right Breast

He looks so confused and frightened, Megan thought as she took Carl's hand. It was like leading a little boy into play. Megan gathered the oranges and found the juicer while Carl stared. His shoulders drooped and his face looked haggard. It was probably not the best time to probe into his past.

"How about I wash the oranges while you squeeze some?" She wanted his participation to keep him busy and to divert him from his thoughts. "A few of these are badly bruised. I hope they're still usable."

Megan washed an orange, then handed it to Carl, who barely remembered to reach out for it. After washing the second orange, Megan turned around to see Carl standing behind her, a whole orange in his hand.

"Let's see. The knives are in this drawer, right?"

Carl came alert and opened the appropriate drawer, which happened to be to the right of the one Megan selected.

"Slow learner," she said, pointing her index finger at her forehead.

When Carl made no move to take out a knife, Megan did. She wasn't sure whether she should cut the orange herself or ask Carl to do it. This decision she didn't have to make, because Carl took the knife from her hand and went to the cutting board, which lay beside the juicer.

Megan felt better now. The buzz from the wine had turned into a mellow glow that warmed her to life and especially to Carl, who suddenly had appeared so vulnerable.

"Want to split an apple turnover with me?"

"With orange juice? Shouldn't we be having milk instead?"

"I guess you're right, but I don't think these oranges will last much longer. The apple turnovers, at least, will last till breakfast."

She continued to wash the oranges and to pass them on to Carl, who sliced and squeezed alternately.

By the time there was enough juice for two glasses, Megan had just about finished rambling on about the first day of her trip and Carl was showing some interest.

"What's your goal on this trip, Megan?"

"To see as much as I can and make friends," she said, clinking her glass into Carl's.

"To our friendship." Carl's eyes were a soft, silky blue that made Megan smile.

"Something wrong with the juice, Megan?"

Carl had just taken a swallow of juice without removing his gaze from her.

Megan felt her cheeks sting and knew she was blushing.

"No. Wait, there's a seed," she said, looking into the liquid.

"Here, let me get it out for you," he said, putting his glass on the table. His callused fingers and abraded palm encircled her hand, which was holding the glass. Smoothly he reached into a nearby drawer and pulled out a spoon. The seed bobbed as Carl immersed the spoon into the juice. Megan giggled while Carl persistently failed to scoop out the seed. She began to think he narrowly missed the accomplishment of his task on purpose as his grasp around her hand became firmer. She was warm and uncomfortable.

"A straw! That's what I need," she said, trying to find some relief from the heat of his nearness.

"I know another way."

Carl brought her hand up toward his lips so that he could take some juice from her glass. Then he lowered her hand and brought his lips to Megan's. Hypnotized by the process, Megan parted her lips. His plush lips barely touched the surface of her own when she felt a trickle of liquid pass into her mouth. Her tongue reached out to lap at the sweet, acidic flavor. His tongue penetrated, sliding across, under, and around her tongue, engaging her in a sensual duel.

After his hand released hers, she could feel the weight of the glass lighten and knew that he was taking the glass from her. Once free of the container, her hand traveled up the length of his shirtsleeve, settling down on one broad shoulder. He pulled her close to his body and pressed her into him. She could feel the fullness of his appetite for her.

Her breath was ragged when he moved from her lips to cover her face with kisses. Her eyes shut to allow his lips to skim her lids. His mouth passed from her lids to her cheek, and then softly reached to the side to nip one of her earlobes.

What was happening? This man was old enough to be her father, but Megan didn't know how to pull away from his hold. He pressed a hand against her buttocks, making her feel dizzy and unsteady. Megan was not a virgin; however, she prided herself on not being easy. She had just met this man and would probably not see him again after tomorrow. Yet as these thoughts swam inside her head, she never attempted to stop his hands as they unknotted the cord around her waist, nor when he pulled open the robe and began exploring summits and an-

gles of her form. Instead, she lowered her hands
from his chest so that he could skim the robe
from her white shoulders. The nubby material
slipped across her sensitive skin, chilling her
while she broiled from within.

He picked her up and carried her from the
kitchen, passing by the closed bedroom door.
Only briefly did Megan recall the hyacinths. Of
course, he would not choose a room that reeked
of the fragrance so attached to a former lover.
Megan pulled closer into the strength of his em-
brace while she undid the buttons on his white
cotton shirt. She slipped a hand across one of
his nipples and sensed a shudder rippling
through his muscles.

Carl placed her down upon an old frayed silk
rug, which lay before the empty fireplace. As
she stretched out, Megan noticed the color of
the faded rug. Had it once been a deep red or a
strong orange? Now it was hard to tell, since the
color appeared to be a strange apricot. Had he
made love with the other woman on this rug?
she wondered. And why had she left such a desirable man? That thought was immediately replaced by the splendor of Carl's naked body
descending upon her. She reached out to accept
him, but he stopped midway to appreciate her
body. She was thrilled by what she saw in his
face. As he stared down, she could see the reflection of her form in his pupils. He seemed
pleased and awed by what he saw. Impishly, she

spread out her limbs so that he couldn't miss a curve or the secret beauty mark just under her right breast. He didn't miss it. Carl touched it, smiled, and licked it lightly with his tongue.

Chapter 11
How Long?

Beverly heard a faint scratching at the bottom of the French doors. She walked to them, pulled back the curtain, and peered down at a brown rat, its claws tapping out a call for entrance. It stopped momentarily to gnaw on a loose piece of wood.

"Sharpening your utensils for dinner, eh, you bugger?"

Her bare foot kicked the bottom of the door, frightening the rat away but causing considerable damage to her first three toes. The skin bulged out and the bones seemed to sink back into gelatinous cartilage.

Beverly squatted down until she barely felt the wooden floor beneath her. Sensations were weakening now. Her nerves, she supposed, were slowly dying. Gently she reached out to

89

touch the damaged toes. She brought one hand up to her lips, kissed the fingers, then lowered the fingers back down to the toes.

"Make it all better," she sadly whispered.

Letting go of her toes, Beverly wrapped her arms around her knees and rocked back and forth. It was so lonely sitting in the house waiting to die. Carl hadn't told her how long it would take. The last time he had seen her, he did say that she couldn't die from a bullet, a knife, or water because she was semi-dead already. Still, he hadn't mentioned fire. Beverly's bloated face creased into fearful lines. Fire. Hardly the way she wanted to go. And what if that couldn't kill her? How would he know when she was dead? When she was nothing but bone or ash?

Beverly looked over at her brass bed and thought of the number of times Carl had shared it with her. She had known he was independent, yet it had always been difficult for him to leave her, except near the end, when she had found it impossible to read him.

How long had he been living this life? she wondered. Should he have died years ago? Did this ritual prevent his aging, or would he have died a young man, unable to do her harm?

"Why didn't you die?" she huffed, her breaths coming in short, rapid spurts.

What of that young girl she had seen him with? Was he lying with her now, memorizing her fine lines and curves? Was the child luxuriating in his passion and prowess?

Beverly reached out and pulled the Amish quilt from the bed. She brought the material to her nose and tried to find his scent, but it was already stale and rancid like the flesh falling from her bones. Holding the quilt to her cheek, she attempted to remember Carl in the beginning of their relationship, his depth, his virility, his warmth and support when she was depressed. The blues always came to her when she was in the midst of writing, but he could banish them easily with one toss on or under the quilt. She hadn't thought she could cry anymore until she saw a few salty dots settle on the material in her hand. They gave her joy in the knowledge that a part of her was still human and alive.

Chapter 12
Ladybug, Right Ankle

After the lovemaking, Carl held Megan briefly, but seemed agitated and withdrawn. Megan wondered whether he was thinking of the hyacinth woman. What had that woman been like and how did she compare to her? She knew she couldn't ask. Not then, not after the immensity of the pleasure they had shared.

Megan let her fingertips travel across his chest and marveled at the balance of his muscles. Not one was out of proportion to the others. He was certainly fit, she thought.

"You'd better get some sleep." He spoke softly and nodded toward the hallway that led to the bedroom.

"I'm comfortable here," she said, knowing he would not enter the bedroom that night, not with the hyacinth odor lingering in the room.

"You won't be in the morning when your bones are aching."

"I'm getting used to that."

"Ah, but I thought that was the reason I had enticed you to stay here." His smile was mischievous.

"Initially." She held her head coyly, wondering whether she could seduce him into another bout of love play.

"O Lord, save me from young, nimble, sexy girls."

"You don't want to be saved. You know that."

"I'm beyond salvation, Megan." His voice was sad, and Megan wondered what she had done or said. Perhaps it was too soon for him to make love again, and she was being too aggressive.

She saw his shirt lying on the floor within reach and grabbed at it.

"What are you doing?"

Demurely, Megan held the shirt up to her breasts.

"Is it okay if I put this on?"

Carl pulled the shirt from her hands, balled it up, and threw it across the room.

"I always want to see you like this. You look best undressed."

"They say most people don't."

"Neither of us is most people, Megan."

She laughed, a little self-conscious about the compliment.

"Will you really let me read your journals, Carl?"

"That would take time, and I thought you were in a hurry to move on."

"If you don't mind, I'd like to stay awhile to read about all the places you've been." *And the other women you have made love with,* she silently added.

"Stay, Megan." Carl ran his hand across her full, round breasts, down her flat abdomen, and across the slender hips. Her thighs held no flab. Her calves bulged from their firmness. Within Megan, there was a rising pride as she stretched out her body.

"What is that?" he asked.

"What?" She followed his gaze until she saw the small dark spot on her right ankle. "Oh, that's my tattoo. One day at school, several us went a bit loony and decided to get one. I got the smallest and least offensive. Sylvia, a friend, got a giant bridal bouquet tattooed on her left buttock. She hoped it would send a hint to her boyfriend. I think it turned him off; he dropped her soon after that."

As she was speaking, Carl had moved down to the tattoo and was fingering the flat ladybug staining her ankle for life. Did he like it, or did he think she was goofy?

"Pretty, isn't it?" She was hoping she could sway his opinion.

Carl spread his hands up her shins and looked at her face.

"Everything about you is pretty."

She tousled his grayish-blond hair and

94

wished he were closer to her age. If he were, would he be as enticing?

Carl started to nibble on the flesh of her abdomen, teasing her, though she was already excited.

"Yes, please," she whispered as he took her again.

Later, a sated Megan rested in Carl's bed without Carl. She was disappointed that he had chosen to go to the study at such a late hour. He claimed he had work to do, but wouldn't disclose to her what the work was.

Megan knew he had traveled and that he kept journals, yet when she mentioned that she had majored in anthropology, he didn't admit to that being his career, although she assumed so. He didn't admit to many things easily, Megan thought.

She looked at the window and was tempted to open it, since the air in the room was oppressive. Barely a hint of hyacinths remained. He lived a simple life, she thought, looking at the one chair in the small room. There were only three pieces of furniture: the chair, the night table, on which sat an art nouveau Tiffany lamp, and the full-size bed on which she lay. No dresser. No armoire. Only a small closet in which she assumed he kept his clothing. The open door to the bathroom revealed a beveled mirror hanging over a very old round pedestal sink. Most things in the house seemed aged. She guessed that he didn't have much money, probably just enough to live out in the woods. Of course, the yellow house downstream was good for some income, but then, he had mentioned repair work that needed to be done on it before it could be rented.

Megan's gaze returned to the closet. The door was painted a glossy off-white like the room's trim. It had a glass doorknob like the ones she remembered in her maternal grandparents' house. When she was five years old, they had died within six months of each other. She never knew the causes of their deaths. Her mother had told her that Grandpa had died from booze and Grandma of a broken heart. That had never satisfied Megan, who had heard the whispers about harlots and suicide. She sighed, thinking about how crazy her family was.

After the reading of the will, her mother had taken her to her grandparents' house to clean out the closets and sell the furnishings. She remembered the thrill of turning doorknobs that looked just like the one in front of her. Behind the doors, there were always exciting, different things to be found, like a dusty stuffed owl, a picture album depicting her mother's childhood from infancy through high-school graduation, and a stitched-up teddy bear, which her mother had allowed her to keep.

It was unlikely that such things would be behind Carl's closet door, but it was still intriguing to fantasize what might be there.

Megan stuck the tip of her right index finger

between her front teeth. Would it hurt anyone if she sneaked a peek? She bit down hard on her finger, punishing herself for the wretched thought. Still the closet, mainly its contents, was intriguing.

She held her breath and sat absolutely still, straining to hear any sound coming from the hallway. There was only silence, except for a few night birds calling to each other outside the window.

Megan threw back the beige sheet and slipped her legs over the side of the bed until her toes touched the faded Persian rug. She tip-toed naked across the room to the closet door.

Maybe it would be locked, she thought, saving her from the despicable crime of being a snoop. She reached out her hand and took a firm hold on the knob, slowly twisted it, finally gave it a little yank, and the door opened.

She glanced over at the door of the bedroom. Still, she heard no sounds within the house. As she pulled the closet door farther, the smell of cedar intensified. When the door was fully open, Megan looked into a cedar-lined closet containing several linen jackets with matching pants. The predominant colors were white and black. There were two dress shirts and a rain-coat huddled together against the side of the closet. Beneath the hanging clothing, Megan spied two cardboard boxes. Both had their flaps firmly interfolded.

Megan bent over and lightly touched the top

of one box. Should she disturb the intricate folds of the cardboard? Would he notice if she did? she wondered while sweeping the palm of her right hand across the top of the boxes. Perhaps his journals were inside. He had offered to let her read them, hadn't he? Knowing that she should wait until Carl handed her the journals, Megan squatted down and started to pull the flaps open while telling herself that she wouldn't read them. She only wanted to be sure they were here. Within seconds the flaps were free and she could peer inside the box at sketch pads.

Megan scratched her head; then she decided to investigate the other box. When the second box was open, she saw more sketch pads piled neatly inside. No journals in either box. Eager to investigate further, Megan looked down at the stained carpet and decided she didn't want to rest her bare bottom on it.

She quietly tiptoed to the kitchen and retrieved the robe from the tile floor. She swung the garment around her shoulders, reaching her long arms into the sleeves. She tied the sash tightly and then silently moved back to the bedroom, pausing in the hallway to verify that the study door was closed. With the bedroom door shut behind her, she hurried to the closet, where she sat in front of the two boxes.

She had planned on not reading the journals, but she did not know what to do with the pads.

Feeling like a sneak, but unable to contain her

curiosity, Megan reached into the first box and removed the top sketch pad. The cover had a few numerical calculations on it. He had obviously been figuring out months and days, but there was no hint as to why. Megan opened the pad and saw a rough draft of a woman's torso. No face, no limbs, just the voluptuous trunk of a woman. The hyacinth woman, Megan guessed. She pulled open the top of the robe to compare herself with the penciled sketch. After checking her own breasts, Megan looked back at the drawing with raised eyebrows. With some disgust, Megan flipped over the page. The next sketch was of limbs in various positions, some of which looked lewd. Eventually, after browsing through several more pages, Megan found the face.

The woman was pretty, with small delicate features, and what looked like a discoloration was shaded in around the left jaw. A birthmark, Megan decided.

So there was the hyacinth woman in bits and pieces. She flashed through more pages, hoping to find the woman sketched out in her entirety. No luck. All of a sudden, Megan realized that the arms and legs she was looking at were not the same ones that had appeared earlier in the pad. No, this person had to be much thinner. With another flip of the page, Megan found a new torso, slight, with small breasts and boyish hips. A few more pages also revealed a new face.

Megan pressed on for another hour, moving

through sketch pad after sketch pad. So many different women, and all unclothed. Every one of the figures had been drawn with a special attention to detail. Only an artist's hand could draw with such precision and realism. Perhaps she had been wrong to assume he was a scientist. No, he must be an artist, she thought. After all, what else could these women be but models?

He was much older than she, Megan reminded herself, and he had never been married. The drawings could be of lovers. Her shoulders shook from an unexpected shiver. Would someone like her someday find Megan stretched out across one of these white sheets of paper?

She pulled the collar of the robe high up around her throat and decided she should leave in the morning. There was nothing she could offer this mysterious man except what all the others had already given.

Megan attempted to return all the pads to their proper order. She didn't know whether there was any specific reason for the way they had been placed in the box, but she wanted to make sure Carl wouldn't suspect her of the act she had committed. Unfortunately, Megan couldn't remember which flap covered which and hoped Carl wouldn't either as she fastened them closed.

Megan rose to her feet, stopping halfway up to allow the knee wound to stretch gradually. When she could place her weight on the injured leg, she closed the closet door. It was stuffy in the room. She unfastened the sash and slipped the robe off, placing it on the chair. With arms outstretched, she went to the window and opened it. She took a deep breath, inhaling the sweetness of the hyacinths, then returned to bed, switching off the light as she climbed in.

Without pulling up the top sheet, Megan plumped up the pillow beneath her head and luxuriated in the comfort and softness of the aroma surrounding her. It seemed to protect and cradle her through her senses. The scent was so loving that it was almost like being a child again and falling asleep in her father's arms.

Suddenly she saw a flash of light at the window. She sat up in the darkened room and peered into the night. Megan recognized Carl's shape walking down the path, flashlight in hand. He seemed to be headed toward the river. Briefly Megan thought about rushing to the window and calling out to him, but then she remembered the sketches. Again she rested her head against the pillow while plumping the down with her hands. It was better to let him go to the river alone. She had already become too involved with this stranger. In the morning she would leave.

Megan smiled as she inhaled the floral perfume of the hyacinths.

Chapter 13
Hyacinths or Rotting Flesh?

Carl had spent forty-five minutes trying to sketch out Megan's torso, but it wasn't working. He did much better on the right foot and ankle and had done an excellent job reproducing the small ladybug just above the anklebone. He didn't remember seeing any other scars or birthmarks, except for the mole under her breast. The wound on her knee appeared to be healing well and probably wouldn't leave any evidence of itself. By the time he needed the full drawing, the cut would have healed. However, for some reason, her torso was causing him some problems. Were the ribs visible? Barely, he thought, but he would have to have another look. Another night. He wasn't up to a second encore performance, he confessed to himself.

After placing the sketch pad in the bottom drawer of his desk, he searched for the key to lock it. Beverly had been at his place only for the signing of the lease; after that, he had made it a point to visit her. That way, he didn't have to worry about her finding anything incriminating. It irked him that he couldn't put Megan in the yellow house until Beverly was gone. He would have to be careful of what he left around. Instinct told him that the young woman could be inquisitive.

Carl pulled open the top drawer of the three-tiered file cabinet. Nothing but old newspaper clippings. He quickly riffled through the smudged newsprint. There wasn't anything that mentioned his name or location, just articles on various missing women he had known. He let the drawer roll back, then went on to the middle drawer. A jumble of keys lay before him. Carl took out the five keys that seemed to be the right size. After trying three of them, he heard the comforting click of the lock. That key was slipped into his pants pocket while the others were tossed back into the drawer. His elbow nudged the drawer and it slammed shut.

Perhaps he should read or listen to music, he thought; however, he felt too edgy. He closed his eyes and tried to visualize Megan's body, the long legs. They were muscular, but not overly so. Her arms were pencil-thin; then again, there was a bit of meat on the upper part of the arm.

Wait, no, that was Beverly, or maybe not.

Carl opened his eyes and slammed his fist on the desk in frustration. "Damn that witch!" he hissed in a hushed voice.

He jumped up, shoved the chair back violently, then stomped out to the hallway, pausing for a few minutes to listen for any movement from where Megan slept. If it hadn't been for those damn hyacinths, he would have been in there memorizing each curve with his hands and eyes even while she slept.

Abruptly he turned toward the front door and strode forward, stopping briefly at the hall closet for the flashlight. He yanked the front door open, but consciously controlled his force when he closed it. He didn't want Megan following him.

Around the back of the house, Carl pulled a shovel out of a dilapidated shed. As he got farther away from the light of the house, he realized that he would be unable to see clearly and switched on the flashlight. His head swiveled around to see his bedroom window. Had he turned on the light too soon? The room was dark, and he saw no one near the window. She was probably exhausted and satisfied and deeply asleep, he thought with a smirk.

Carl found the path and started down toward the river, veering off midway toward Beverly's grave. He could feel the bile rolling around in his stomach as the hideous floral odor intensified when he got closer to her grave.

"We'll see what you're up to, bitch," he muttered as he threw the shovel down on the ground. He placed the flashlight on a large rock behind him, undid the buttons on the cuffs of his sleeves, and started to roll the soft cotton material up his arms, first one, then the other.

When he was finished, Carl picked up the shovel and started to dig into the mound that covered Beverly's coffin. There was a breeze, but it couldn't dry up all the perspiration flowing down Carl's face as he dug with tremendous energy, trying to unearth Beverly's secret hold over him. Several times Carl swallowed down the contents of his stomach as the smell of the hyacinths intensified the deeper he dug. His arms vibrated when the shovel hit the hard surface of the coffin. This encouraged him to work faster as he cleared all the dirt from the wooden surface.

Once he could completely see the top of the coffin, Carl stood straight and looked up to see the treetops and the stars pressed against the night sky. Compacted earth surrounded him and that horrendous flower seemed to steal what air there was from him.

With difficulty Carl climbed out of the grave. Taking four paces to the rock, he retrieved his flashlight, then turned back to the grave and retraced his steps.

"So what am I going to find, Beverly? A hothouse full of fresh hyacinths or rotting flesh?" He knew what he wanted to find, but feared that was not to be. "How did you defeat me?"

Carl shook his head. No, she couldn't have defeated him, not yet. The shiver of death did not chill him. His body was still strong. He didn't feel the chewing maggots inside his gut.

"No, Beverly, you haven't defeated me at all, have you?"

He rested the flashlight on the edge of the hole he had dug and jumped back into the grave. He pushed his back against one earthen wall and swung the lid of the coffin open.

The putrid, stale smell of decaying flesh brought a smile to his wet face. Even in his joy Carl couldn't prevent himself from gagging. His throat burned; he had swallowed his gastric juices so many times that he thought he would never be able to eat again.

Once he had his body's response under control, he looked in at the drawing. In the half-light from the flashlight he saw the paper frayed at the edges. The pulp was turning a beige-brown, as if it had been carelessly left near a flame. The lines that made up the drawing seemed to be coming apart. Disintegration was almost imperceptible, but Carl could see the subtle breaks.

"So where are your pretty hyacinths, Beverly?" Carl reached up to the edge of the grave and grasped the flashlight. He drew the bright light across the decaying rose petals on which the drawing rested. "No garden here for you to fuss over." Carl laughed loudly, his shoulders shook, and the light bounced off the dirt walls.

Abruptly he stopped. Something cool and wet slithered across the back of his neck. Quickly Carl raised his free hand to the collar of his shirt and traced the creased edge to the back. When he reached approximately midway, he shifted his hand to his neck. Slowly he drew his hand upward until he held a squiggling chunk, then pulled it off, bringing it forth into the illumination of the flashlight.

The worm wiggled and squirmed on his palm under the intensity of the bulb. Carl turned his palm downward and shook his hand until the worm fell onto the drawing.

He closed the lid of the coffin, placed the flashlight aboveground, then climbed out. He rubbed the palm on which the worm had been against his denim jeans. His blisters had reopened, leaving a trail of blood across the material.

The stench of Beverly's flesh was gone, replaced by the hyacinths' perfume. Carl's nostrils flared as he picked up the shovel and started tossing the dirt back into the grave. He firmly packed the dirt into the hole. He'd allow no escape for Beverly, no reprieve from death.

When he was finished, Carl pulled down his right shirtsleeve, then drew the arm across his face, sopping up the salty sweat. A harder and more important job lay ahead of him, but first he would return to the house for some sleep. In the morning he would increase his efforts to duplicate Megan. He had the feeling that he would need her services soon.

Chapter 14
Prayer

Beverly felt a terrible tingling sensation traveling up and across her body. The nerves embedded in her decaying skin were more alive than she had realized, and they were now dancing wildly. She flattened herself against the solid wood floor and began to writhe to the soundless music.

"Oh God, stop this. Please. Please," she begged.

It felt as if something heavy and wet were crawling across her body, weighing it down. She began to scrape at her chest, stomach, abdomen, and finally her thighs, picking off the invisible intruder.

Eventually her body went limp and a numbness settled upon her. A few minutes passed before she brought her hands up to her face, resting her prayerful fingers against her lips. Never had she been religious, but as a young child her parents had sent her to Sunday school, more out of duty than from any real belief. She tried to recall a prayer.

"Our Father, Who art in Heaven, hallowed be Thy name," she began, and she found as she progressed that the words came more easily to her.

As she whispered the word "Amen," Beverly looked down at what was left of her long fingernails and saw bits of flesh embedded inside them. She turned the palms of her hands toward her face. One nail was missing; another hung by a thread; the others were thick with the stench of her demise.

Beverly sat up with palms outstretched in front of her. These hands did not belong to her. She looked at her breasts, which were shriveled and hung down as if her nipples were tiny weights. The hands lifted the breasts, and as they did, she spied the gashes she herself had inflicted only minutes before. The breasts were foreign to her, as were the other parts of this thing that sat in her place.

Carl stole my body, incorporated it into his own cells so that he could entice and charm young girls, she thought. So that he could survive beyond her.

"I want myself back, Carl," she hissed under the glow of a moon that penetrated the glass of the French doors.

Chapter 15
Hyacinth Girl

Megan turned over onto her side and into the glare of the noontime sun. Immediately she pulled the sheet over her head. Then the strangeness of her surroundings began to seep into her consciousness. She was not lying comfortably on her own mattress. This was not one of the pastel sheets she owned; instead, it was a dingy beige. Only a man would buy such a bland color, she thought. A man! Where the heck was she?

She threw off the covers, sat up, and looked around the room. The wicker chair, the nightstand with the art nouveau lamp, and, yes, that sweet perfume of the hyacinths: this was Carl's abode. She blushed, remembering her last encounter with the older man. A pretty smile perked up her rosy cheeks, but as she slipped out of bed, her glance shifted to the small closet with the glass doorknob, and all of the torsos, limbs, and faces returned to her memory.

"I've got to get out of here before I get in too deep," she muttered as she padded her way across the faded Persian rug toward the bathroom. For a second she halted, wondering whether she should close the window before taking her shower; after all, it would take a while for the fragrance of the hyacinth to fade. Odd, she thought, that a flower could so permeate a room, and she hadn't remembered seeing even a single one outside the window.

Megan shrugged and went through the bathroom doorway. She would deal with the window later. By the position of the sun, she assumed it was late, and she wanted to be gone from this place before evening. She turned around and peeked back into the bedroom, searching the walls and nightstand for a clock. None. *Guess when one lives out in the woods one doesn't worry about time,* she thought. She took a step back and closed the bathroom door.

A half hour later, Megan, wrapped in the navy robe, was tiptoeing down the hallway to the living room. She thought that she remembered seeing her backpack lying on the floor alongside some wood that was probably meant for the fireplace. There it was, exactly where she had seen it the night before when Carl had carried her into the room.

She snatched it up and practically ran back

to the bedroom. She had a change of clothes in the pack that she could put on before she went into the backyard to retrieve the clothes she had washed the day before. Quickly she slipped on her bikini underwear, pulled some baggy jeans over them, then fetched a white T-shirt out of the pack.

The T-shirt was almost over her head when she heard the door open. She pulled the shirt down as fast as she could, and turned to see Carl standing in the hallway, a half-smile on his face, in appreciation for what was before him.

"I've got to be going," she said. "If you don't mind, I'll just grab some fruit and refill my canteen with some tap water."

Carl's lips tightened into a straight line.

"Oh, yes. Don't let me forget my clothes in the backyard."

He continued to stand just beyond the bedroom threshold. Remembering the window, she thought, *With this guy hyacinths are just as good as garlic is with vampires*. She wondered whether she should continue the standoff or close the window. Megan glanced at the bed and thought, *Naw, even with the window closed the fragrance will last for a while*. She may as well close it.

"It got stuffy last night, so I opened the window," she said as she approached the breeze blowing into the room. Before closing the window, she took a quick gander at the yard to see if she could spot any hyacinths. Not a one in sight. The window was sticking again, as it had the previous night. *Oh, no! Not another scene like what occurred then, please.* Megan pushed with all her strength until the window fell, and she heard the glass shatter.

She gave a long, guttural moan and leaned her head against the windowframe.

"I'll pick up the pieces of glass," she said as she raised her head. "I'm sorry. It was stuck, and I guess I pushed too hard." Megan saw the broken window cord and thought that it probably had needed to be fixed for some time. It wouldn't have happened if he had taken better care of his place. She knew she couldn't say that to him, though.

"If you have a broom and—" Megan swung around. She couldn't see him from where she stood, but was surprised that he hadn't stuck in his head to see what had happened. Out of all those women, the hyacinth gal must have been something, to cause this response to her flowers.

Megan walked over to the doorway. The hallway was empty. Her eyebrows lifted in surprise. Guided by common sense, she found the broom, dustpan, and an empty brown paper bag in the pantry closet in the kitchen. She passed no one in the hallway on her way back to the bedroom.

After placing all the broken glass that she could find in the paper bag, she returned to the kitchen to deposit it in the trash can under the sink.

She carried her backpack over one shoulder, removed the canteen from the pack, and refilled it. Then she stuffed several apples and the canteen inside the bursting pack.

"How am I ever going to fit the extra clothes inside?" She pressed down on the springy contents, then dropped the backpack on a kitchen chair and went out the door to the yard.

Her clothes were gone. Could an animal have taken them during the night? she wondered. Megan stomped the dirt with both feet.

"Didn't we agree that you looked better without these things?"

Turning to her right, Megan spied Carl leaning against an old shed. In his hands were her clothes.

"I wouldn't be welcome in civilized company without them."

"I'm not civilized," he said, and casually flipped her clothes through a paneless window of the shed.

"Ah, come on. I just washed those things." The shed looked filthy from the outside, and Megan figured the inside wouldn't look any better.

Megan marched to the door of the shed. It was padlocked.

"No joking around, Carl. I want my clothes now." She stomped her right foot for emphasis.

"You told me you would stay, Megan."

She didn't want to admit that she had been nosing around in the boxes.

"Life's too short to stop at any one place for too long, Carl. I have to be on my way."

"Why are you leaving? Did I frighten you?"

That sounded like a good out, but his expression was so sad that she couldn't use it.

"No, Carl. We're too different and—"

"I'm too old."

"No! I found you fascinating and was dying to see the journals you told me about."

"Didn't I meet your expectations last night?"

Uh-oh. This was getting sticky. She had planned to avoid the topic of sex altogether.

Her cheeks were burning. "Actually, you were the best lover I've ever had." She needn't tell him she had been with only two other guys.

"Why leave?"

He said so damn little; yet it was so difficult to walk away.

"Because I doubt I could ever compare with . . ." There was a moment's pause; she had to be careful here. "With your previous relationships."

"How can you say that when you know nothing about my past?"

"I know about the hyacinth woman." Megan saw Carl's body tense. "Sorry, I didn't mean to bring her up again. Obviously she hurt you very badly."

"No, she's the one who suffers," he said placidly.

"But you're stuck here with her memories, while she's moved on with her life."

"She gave me something special, Megan, and I wouldn't have given up my experiences with her for any trail that might take me away from here."

"Sometimes it's better to leave before you get hurt."

"How could she hurt me? She loved me."

"But now you can't stand a beautiful flower just because it was this woman's favorite. That comes from pain."

"I won, Megan. I'm still here. She's the one who had to go."

"You think I'm running away, too, don't you? You think I'm afraid of you and my feelings."

"Afraid of your feelings for me. I don't believe you're afraid of me."

Megan chewed her bottom lip. Should she confront him about the sketch pads? Maybe he'd have a reasonable answer. Perhaps he hadn't had one sex orgy after another. *Listen to yourself, Megan. When did you become a prude?*

"Carl, I couldn't sleep last night."

He smiled. "I would have thought you were exhausted."

Her cheeks didn't sting. Maybe she was getting used to his innuendos.

"There was nothing to read, and I didn't want to disturb you, since you had sounded so keen on working. I thought you might have had some important project to complete." Megan saw Carl's head nod. "So I kind of have this thing about doorknobs. My grandparents had glass doorknobs on all their doors." She was dragging this out. He'd be dozing by the time she finished. "So I noticed that your bedroom closet had a glass doorknob." His body stiffened. *You're in for it now,* thought Megan, but she couldn't stop. "I opened your closet and found the boxes."

"You opened them."

"Yeah." Her head was bobbing. She felt like a car ornament. "I sort of flipped up the flaps and noticed all those sketch pads."

Carl's eyes were no longer a clear blue; they seemed muddied by anger. *Oops,* she thought. Maybe honesty was not the best policy.

"I guess you're an artist." He was too angry about what she had found to be an artist, but she wanted to give him an easy way out.

"No."

Megan's eyes widened. The lecher was going to admit to all of his philandering.

"The woman who planted the flowers was the artist. She left piles of her work behind. I was emotionally unable to discard them."

"You mean the hyacinth girl drew all those naked women?"

"She left me for one of her models."

Megan's heart sank. How could she be so cruel as to bring up all these bad associations? Yet a single doubt lingered.

"This place is so out of the way. How did she get models to come this far?"

"We didn't always live here. We moved here

toward the end of our relationship. Her last model followed us and posed down near the water several times."

Near where the hyacinths grow, no doubt, Megan concluded.

"I'm sorry, Carl. I wish I hadn't brought any of this up. You look so pained. What can I do to help?"

"Stay, Megan. Please."

Chapter 16
A Taste of Death

The twit was going to accept the explanation, Carl could tell. Tears were gathering in the corners of her eyes. *Come on, Megan, say yes. Agree to stay, at least for a few days.*

Carl played it like Russian roulette. Of course, with his strength he could physically prevent Megan from leaving, but that wouldn't set him free from guilt. He needed her consent, her collaboration in the deed even if the final outcome was unknown to her. Carl hoped it never got to the point when he would be forced to drug and tie someone down, because he didn't think he could do that. No, he would die then, for it would be time.

"I'll stay, Carl, only to keep you company. We won't make love again. I don't think either of us is ready for that kind of commitment."

That resolution won't last long, Carl thought. He knew she would change her mind. She was obviously malleable and naive.

"But I'll only stay for another week, two weeks at the most. Understand?"

Carl smiled; a few days would be all he needed.

"I understand, Megan. I wouldn't force you to stay if you really wanted to move on, but I think it is too soon for both of us to part."

"Sorry about the window. Is there some place we can go to get a new pane? I'll pay for it."

"Don't worry about the window. I'll go into town later this afternoon."

"Great! I must have passed by it somehow. Maybe we can have dinner there. Is there a decent restaurant?"

"I'm afraid it's rather small and boring. Nothing there would interest a young girl like you. Why don't I give you some of my journals to read while I'm away? Believe me, they would be a lot more interesting than the hardware store."

Megan's bottom lip protruded in a sulky pout, but Carl didn't want anyone to know she was there. Already he would have to tell the local merchants that his tenant had to leave suddenly because of illness in the family. Everyone knew Beverly had a brother with a drinking problem, who could conveniently have had a bad attack of cirrhosis.

Carl rubbed the back of his index finger across Megan's bottom lip. Her lips started to pucker before she pulled back her head.

"So where are the journals?"

"In the study." Carl dropped his hand to his side. As he turned toward the house, he felt Megan's hand grab his left forearm. He looked at her inquisitively.

"My clothes are in that filthy shed." Her tight fist waved back and forth while her thumb extended in the direction of the shed. "I hope you still have the key, because I don't think either of us would care to crawl through the window."

"It's not locked."

"What do you mean? There's a padlock on the front door."

Carl went over to the shed and lifted the door off the rusted hinges.

"You know, Carl, you mentioned fixing up that rental place down the river. Ummm, have you given any thought to starting here first? I used to help my dad sometimes, although I guess I acted more like a gofer than a repairperson. Still, I did spend a lot of time watching him and could probably be very helpful."

He laughed. She definitely would be helpful. She'd save his life. Carl went into the shed and found Megan's clothes lying on top of some old newspapers. When he lifted her jeans, he saw a black widow spider scurry down the side of the yellowed newspapers. Cautiously, he lifted her denim shirt. Nothing moved, but he shook both garments out to make sure they were free of vermin.

"Megan, it might be better if you didn't poke around in this shed," he said, crossing the threshold. He handed the clothing to her. "Lucky there are no glass doorknobs to intrigue you here." Carl replaced the door on the orange-brown hinges.

"Sorry about that, too. I shouldn't have been so nosy, but you can trust in one thing, and that's that there's no way I'm going to pry into that mess . . . or whatever you have stored in that shed. It has no appeal for me."

Carl decided to shift the last journal from under the back porch to the shed.

"I guess they don't need another washing," she said, inspecting the faded blue material in her hands.

Megan was holding her jeans up in the air. The shirt hung over one of her extended arms. She shook the jeans violently.

"I did that already, Megan." Then, to ensure that Megan would not be drawn to the shed, he added, "After I found the black widow under them."

The jeans almost fell from her hands.

"Thank you, Carl. Did you check the pockets, too?"

Carl watched Megan squeeze the outside material of the pockets together tightly. She gingerly used one hand to open the slit of the pocket so that she could peek inside.

"Any squished arachnids?"

"Spiders always give me the queasies, with

their long legs and sticky webs. Did you know that for mobility they make parachutes and blow around in the wind?" Megan's shoulders visibly shivered. "Never mind. I don't want to think about it."

"What kind of archaeologist would you make?"

"Well, Indiana Jones was afraid of snakes."

"It's getting late. If I'm going to go into town, I had better leave soon." Carl could hear her stomach growl. "Seems like you frequently forget to have your meals."

Megan must have decided that her clothes were safe, because she hugged them close to her body.

"I had planned on stopping down the road from here. I was going to have some dried beef and an apple."

"How about some waffles with strawberries and cream, instead?"

Megan nodded enthusiastically.

"You'll have to make them yourself, though, because I've got to go. I left some batter in the refrigerator and the waffle iron is still on the kitchen counter, cleaned and ready to use. Don't mind eating alone, do you?"

"No, but I feel terrible; after all, it's because of me that you have to go into town."

"It's all right. I'll pick up some supplies while I'm there."

"Oh, and the journals?"

"I'll leave one on top of the desk in the study."

A contented Megan strolled back to the

house, with Carl behind her examining the texture and fall of her red, curly tresses.

Carl left Megan bouncing about in the kitchen, preparing her brunch. He had left one of his early journals on his desk. It was thick and should entertain her until he got back.

After pushing the boat into the water and hopping in, he checked his wristwatch. Just enough time to make it to the hardware store. As he rowed down the river, he thought of Beverly. How was she? he wondered. He had buried her drawing deep, but he knew the rate of decay varied with each person. Carl had been unable to judge from the drawing the night before, because he had never dug up any of the previous coffins.

When a hint of the yellow and white house could be seen beyond the trees, Carl moved his boat inland without thinking. It was as if the green-grass-covered earth were a magnet and the shell of his boat were iron instead of wood.

He slipped his shoes off and rolled up the trouser legs, then stepped into the water, dragging the boat next to him. Carl let go of the boat once they both were firmly on land. Not bothering to roll down his trousers or to put on his shoes, Carl set out toward the house.

As soon as he entered the back garden, the hyacinth smell encircled him. This time the flowers were real, and he did not feel the same repulsion that he had experienced back at his home. Smiling, he fingered one of the blue-purple flowers while thinking how harmless they were. Perhaps he should pick a few and bring them back to Megan. She would like that. Megan wasn't so bad when she wasn't getting into mischief. Certainly she had the womanly charms that he enjoyed, even if the child in her sometimes angered him.

Carl heard a click and knew it was the French doors being opened behind him. He had almost emptied his mind of Beverly with the fresh sparkle of Megan's youth. There was a rasping noise that sounded almost like a cough. When he heard it again, he realized that it had not been a cough but his own name being wheezed out from someone's chest. His hand circled the flower, slowly squeezing it in his fist. His wrist made a quick snapping movement, and the crushed flower was free of its stem. Again, the sound pressed into the warm afternoon air, forcing him to hear the wave of pain that it carried. The tight fist opened and he looked at the flower he had destroyed, permanently useless as a beautiful object of nature. But it could fertilize the earth and give life to other plants. Carl sprinkled the petals onto the ground. Most of them settled across his bare toes.

Again, the air seemed heavy with the wilted cry that he could barely recognize as his own name. Why had she not come to him? What was her purpose in beckoning him? There was no salvation for her now; he was sure she was too far gone. He thought of turning back to the side gate and exiting the garden without acknowledging her plea. Yes, it was a plea. Even with the distortion in her voice, he could tell it was a cry out to him. What for? Did she simply want to remind him of what he had left behind in this house? Well, she did that every second of the day, whether she knew it or not.

"What is it, Beverly?" he asked without moving his head.

The only reply was that twisted sound echoing out of a decaying hole that once was a mouth.

"I can't stay with you, Beverly. There are errands I must run in town. I merely stopped by . . ." He hesitated. Why had he returned now to this house? "On impulse," he stated without lying.

Again, the terrible pressure of his name being pushed forward through the heat of the sun's rays.

He turned. It was still Beverly. Remnants of her beauty lasted in the aura circling her form. Her breasts, though, hung low over a bloated stomach. The abdomen was distended, and her sex was lost among loose flesh. The once-slender legs were now scrawny with purple splotches dotting what was left of her skin. There were tears in the flesh covering her limbs. A muscle protruded across her right forearm, and he watched the muscle weakly flex as she raised her hand to him. His stare traveled up to her face. The eye sockets loosely held her dark pupils; the bridge of her nose seemed flattened, the lips swollen but retracted over teeth that protruded from recessed gums. He watched her tongue move as she pronounced his name over and over.

Mesmerized, Carl moved closer to Beverly. The stink of her body made him pause as he squinted against the invisible sulfurous air. Still he saw her, not as his corpse but as his loving Beverly, who would greet his desires with the fulsomeness of her spirit. Her tongue called out his name, drawing him closer. Blocking his senses, his mind guided his body forward toward her outstretched arms.

As he crossed the threshold and moved into her bedroom, Carl felt her fingers touching the back of his head, mingling those craggy appendages with his silken, silvery gold hair.

"Caaarl," the voice called, and he heard the deep intake of air that whistled through her larynx.

He moved with her as she pulled him back to the bed. When she let herself fall backward on top of the bare mattress, he followed. No, he couldn't break the hold death and life had over him.

He lowered his mouth upon the gaping hole through which she wheezed and smelled the sourness of her breath. Their tongues met, hers parched, his wet with anticipation. His torso rested against the blubber under him and his hands searched the flaccid breasts as if for mother's milk.

His spine tingled as she drew her nails across the back of his cotton shirt. He felt her hands disappear between their bodies and he lifted up enough to allow them to undo his trousers. He was tasting his own death and was ready to enter it safely, securely, without the permanency he feared.

The miasma of Beverly's body seduced Carl, whose rigid manhood lasciviously sought entrance into her decomposing temple.

Carl felt the jolt of her body beneath him. She tried to pull her mouth away from his, stealing the thrill that once had been within his grasp. *No!* his mind cried as he held on tightly, managing to slide into her feminine orifice. His foreskin chafed against her walls, which with the continuous massaging motion broke down into a silky, bloody sludge, titillating his passion.

"Take my life, take my seed," he cried out as he spilled his molten sperm inside her.

Chapter 17
A Bouquet of Hyacinths

Megan slathered whipped cream over her golden waffles, then dropped five or six strawberries randomly on top, adding a quick dollop of cream as a finale. This was far better than what she had planned for that afternoon's meal.

After carrying the plate to the table, Megan left the kitchen to retrieve Carl's journal from the study. There it was, sitting on top of a dark-green blotter. When she picked up the book, her glance casually took in what appeared to be a rough draft of a profile on the right upper corner of the green felt. Not very good, she mused. Nothing like the work contained in the sketch pads. *Good try, Carl, but no go.* Megan chuckled and returned to the kitchen. She propped the book up against an empty cookie jar. Her behind plopped down upon the wooden slats of the chair.

She noticed that the cover of the journal was a tad weathered, with old water stains dripping down the edges. It must have gotten caught in the rain once or twice, she thought. Carefully she lifted the hard cover, then rested it gently back against the glass container. The handwriting could be described as neat scrawl. Not a single letter strayed below or above its proper space; however, the rounded letters sometimes took on messy loops and lines.

"I'm going to have to get used to your handwriting before I can seriously sit down and read this stuff."

Using her utensils, Megan began chomping into her food. Heaven, she thought, as sugary clouds of cream collided with a ripe burst of strawberry.

Again, her eyes passed over the first page of the journal, and she realized she was looking at dates and names of people and places, along with what seemed to be temperatures. No doubt this was some sort of index Carl had used so that he could locate data easily.

She recognized none of the people's names, or the places except for Rio de Janeiro. *I guess I'm a dunce when it comes to geography,* she admitted.

By the time she had finished her meal, she was able to decipher most of Carl's script.

Maybe it was because her penmanship was not the best either; still, she was glad that she would be able to read it through without having to question Carl about whether something was an *a* or an *o*.

Megan washed the plates she had used and quickly ran a sponge across the table, being careful not to touch the journal, although she imagined that Carl would never notice another water stain among the conglomeration already there.

So now where should she go to read? There was Carl's study, but even during daylight it seemed to be dingy there. The bedroom was off-limits. She always fell asleep reading in bed, and somehow the kitchen didn't seem appropriate.

After picking up the book, Megan moved to the living room, where she still didn't feel comfortable. She tried the Afghan-covered couch, but felt round springs poke into her derriere. Sliding down onto the faded silk rug, Megan leaned her back against the couch, bent her knees, and rested the journal against her upper thighs. She opened the book and leafed through the pages, trying to gauge how long it would take to finish it.

Slowly a ray of sunlight coming from the window moved across her hand. Megan looked up at the window and decided that she should be outdoors. Immediately she made for the front door and fresh air.

As she rambled down the path toward the river, she caught the scent of hyacinths and decided to scout around for the flower.

Once off the trail, Megan squinted into the sun, trying to detect the hyacinths, which by the aroma had to be nearby. None was to be seen, and she would have kept on wandering if she hadn't tripped on several splintered wooden sticks. She caught herself, but it didn't save her from her own chastisement.

"There I go again. Just when one booboo is healing, I'm ready to replace it with another."

When she looked down, she saw a rectangular mound, something like what she had seen in the cemetery shortly after her father had been buried.

Megan, get a grip. Do you think Carl buried his hyacinth woman out here? Besides, he's already told you that she left with a model. She shook her head, as if that would shake the idea from her mind.

Her eyes searched the landscape but could see only old, dead foliage from some flowers, although there didn't appear to be any flowering plants in the vicinity. Megan shrugged and moved away, hoping to locate the hyacinths. The odor of the flowers became vague as she moved. She decided to retrace her steps.

As she returned to the earthen mound, she noticed the fragrance was at its peak. The dead flowers nearby didn't resemble hyacinths, and, besides, she reasoned, they were dead and couldn't emit that sweet odor.

Without thinking, Megan stood on top of the mound where the smell of hyacinths was most intense. Suddenly she sensed that the soil beneath her feet was liquefying. Quickly she leaped to the side, turning to look back once her feet were back on solid earth.

For a second the soil seemed to be breathing, inhaling and exhaling in a heavy, hushed panting. Then it was still.

"How can soil breathe?" Megan grumbled. Could there have been a mild earthquake, one that affected only a single plot of earth? No way! Was it possible for someone to hallucinate after having had too much sleep, the same as when you had too little? she wondered.

Megan paced the length and width of the mound, staring at it, defying it to move again. The grass grew tall around the plot. She hated thinking of it in terms of a plot, but that was what it appeared to be. Carl could have buried a favorite pet here, although there was nothing in the house that suggested he had ever had a pet. Besides, his personality didn't mesh with that of a dog or cat owner. Perhaps he had one of those exotic talking parrots from the jungle.

"There's got to be a good reason for this." She sat beside the mound and let her right hand pat it. "It must have been a large pet." She had doubted him before and had made a fool of herself. "Maybe he was digging a well or building a new shed." All improbable, but so was the idea that he had buried a human being here.

Megan scratched away some of the topsoil from the mound, then stopped to pick up one of the splintered sticks lying nearby. After several pokes with the stick, the pockmarked mound looked almost the same. No liquefaction, no feathers from a once-squawking parrot, and no limb pushing up out of the ground. She had read about dead bodies occasionally surfacing if not buried deep enough. But, she told herself, there was no body to rise up here. Yet there was something curious about . . . *Megan, read your book and mind your own business*, she commanded.

Listening to what she thought was her better judgment, she dropped the stick and flipped open the book. It was as good a place as any to read. There was fresh air mixed with the scent of hyacinth and an oak tree that offered some shade from the afternoon sun. Thus Megan joined Carl's trip down the Amazon in a slender boat, with a guide and two hired laborers.

Initially Megan followed Carl on the laborious land route into the jungle and waited with him for several weeks in a small village until the river swelled from the rains. Later she stopped with him in a village built near the Amazon. There they celebrated his arrival with a *chicha* drinking session. A few paragraphs later, she learned that the beverage was made of corn and copious amounts of saliva donated by the village virgins in order to bring about fermentation.

At this point, Megan's nose wrinkled.

"Can you believe that! What about hygiene? I know they're virgins, but still, who knows what horrid germs could be lurking in their saliva?" Megan's head turned from the book so that she could look over at the mound. "What am I doing talking to a clump of earth? It smells nice, but I'm certainly not going to get any entertaining conversation back. Oh, Carl, where are you?"

Megan had read enough to be prepared to interrogate the traveler if he ever returned. She forced herself back into deciphering Carl's handwriting and continued to read until she heard some distant splashing.

"Carl," she shouted as she rose to her feet. She ran back to the dirt path with the book grasped tightly in her left hand. Just as she appeared from out of the shrubbery, Carl was turning the near bend and seemed startled by her appearance.

"Megan, were you able to see me from the house?"

"Well, not—"

"You must have been wondering when I'd be back."

"As a matter of fact, I was starting to get a—"

"For you," he said, bringing a bouquet of hyacinths from behind him. His eyes sparkled, and his face almost appeared unlined from the happiness lighting his expression.

"You went back to the rental house. Did you

do some work?" Megan took the flowers, cradling them in her arms.

"I believe I've managed to resolve a problem that existed for me there. And what have you been doing?"

"Besides gorging on waffles, you mean?"

"On you, they look good," he said lewdly.

"Not as many as I had." Beneath the mask of her denial was an invitation to explore her body to find out who was right.

Megan had never heard Carl laugh so freely. What could he have managed to straighten out? It must have been a heavy-duty plumbing problem, she thought. For a split second, Megan glanced back at the mound and thought of asking about it, but it could only ruin the mood, she knew. She took Carl's arm and started back to the house with him.

"The windowpane?"

"I didn't make it into town. I'll go tomorrow or the next day. Luckily, the nights are warm."

"But the scent?"

Carl leaned over and sniffed the budding hyacinths cuddled in her arms. "Lovely, aren't they?"

Panic hit Megan. Could she refuse this man? Would her resolve to keep the relationship platonic be washed away?

Chapter 18
Jealousy

She lay with splayed legs across the black and gray quilting of the mattress. Stunned. Resigned. Her bald head lifted slightly to glimpse her own trunk. The wasted flesh looked singed under the passing twilight. She didn't remember looking like this when he had first taken her. On that day, there had been a bright afternoon sun that heated the loins of both lovers.

There was a cackle. She heard it inside her head. A wry kind of sound, the echo of humor mated with malice. She heard it again and felt the fetid air cross her lips. Her head sank back down upon the rough ticking of her bed, of her grave. *It should be white satin*, she thought, *with a splash of red roses circling her body.*

A low, gravelly chuckle baited her. It snickered in her ears and vibrated through her lips.

Then she was still again, with only the thin, fading light of day moving in the room. Dwindling sunlight sought out forgotten corners of the room as if attempting to hide from the moon's pale light.

Beverly closed her eyes. She didn't want to watch the sun's slow death.

"Stop and rest," she whispered to the sun. "You can't escape the final blackness. Don't move. Let night lie down on you and infuse itself into you. Receive it like a sacrament, so that it can be passed on and given back again."

Another cackle scratched her throat. The sound had shaved off an infinitesimal number of cells, and she had none to spare for frivolous mirth. She had to learn how to control the wizened woman growing inside of her. Had Carl impregnated her with that hag, or had the witch grown out of Beverly's wasted cells? Ovum, sperm combined to wreak the havoc she must preside over. Yet how could she give birth when she had nothing with which to suckle?

A hideous, muffled wail issued forth between rotting teeth, a cry that only she could hear.

A name formed upon her lips, and she tried to pronounce it aloud. Her purplish tongue slipped, each time losing its proper position. However, Beverly kept trying. Her eyes opened wide. Was the girl's scent on him? Everything was so vague now; she could barely touch reality. Yet she knew that he had brought the girl with him, on his clothes, in his hair, lingering on his skin. The girl was there. Beverly's nails splintered on the mattress as she dug into the feathered stuffing. He brought the girl to torment her. As he grunted out his convulsive movements, he had panted out her own name, not the girl's, but he knew he stank of adolescence. A harridan's laugh seized her thoughts; a blankness enveloped the few moments until the shrew was contained.

She must be there with him. Did he stop at the river to wash the death from his cock, or did he bring it back to the youth? Could the girl smell the virago scent? she wondered. *Essence of death, my dear, given to me by* . . . Here her mind faltered. The name she tried to say, tried to call.

"Carl," the old woman within her cried out. "Carl, Carl, Carl. And he will share the gift with you, little girl, when old Beverly is done with it."

A shiver on the surface of the mattress took Beverly back to the tormenting darkness of her bedroom. The sun had given up with the call of his name. Another shiver, closer to her now. Only a slight quiver through the ticking, but still it was closer than before.

The rat froze as Beverly raised her head, the outline of its body haloed by the moon. Its bright, round eyes stared back into Beverly's sunken orbs.

"So you want a bite, my dear. Here, try some," she shrieked as she struck the rat hard with the decaying side of her right leg.

The rat fell backward, landing on its feet; it scurried across the floor and through the French doors, which Carl had left open. The rodent ran fast from the gurgled laughter behind it.

Chapter 19
Seduction

Carl gave her flowers and aggressive stares. The seduction had begun. Should she? Shouldn't she? Megan had decided that she wouldn't make love with Carl again. She had made the decision that morning when she had also decided to stay a week or two longer with him. She knew that she should keep to that spoken determination if she wanted to be able to leave without looking back or perhaps lingering for much longer than she should. Of course, Carl might tire of her first and encourage her to move on. Still, she couldn't rely upon that, and, besides, if that happened, she would be heartbroken. No, she had to keep her distance, perhaps find other ways to entertain him. The book would be perfect. They could spend hours talking about his journey.

Carl's hand slipped around her waist, and she felt him pulling her closer to his side as they walked.

"I've managed to read several chapters of your journal, and I've got tons of questions to ask. Do you have any of the Tupi earthenware that you wrote about in the book?"

Megan scrambled through a multitude of questions, and Carl listened in silence. He didn't appear annoyed at her blabbering. Whatever he had accomplished had put him in a super mood, she thought as she confidently continued her avalanche of words.

Once inside the house, Carl found a vase for the hyacinths and gave it to her. He headed for the kitchen with Megan straggling along behind, lips moving constantly and arms loaded with flowers, vase, and book.

"At first, I had some difficulty deciphering your handwriting, but then I got used to it."

"Used to it?" he asked.

"Now I can read it without too much scratching of the head," she said, giggling.

Carl, who had been so happy before, suddenly turned around and faced Megan.

"My handwriting is easy to read."

A statement that demanded that she agree. Megan promptly nodded, amazed by the quick change in Carl.

He smiled. "Want to help me make dinner again?"

Another swift flip-flop, she noted.

"I should make dinner. Here I am intruding and—"

"No. No, it's fun to work together in the kitchen. Maybe we could even take turns talking. You might even get a few answers to all the questions you posed."

Megan laughed, embarrassed by her presumption that once inside the house he would want to bed her immediately.

"Sorry, I guess I was so excited to have you back that I overdid it a little."

"A lot."

He was honest, she thought.

Carl assisted her by relieving her of the book, which he tossed onto the kitchen counter. Megan laid the flowers on the table and then went to the faucet to fill the vase.

"It was nice of you to bring the flowers back," she said as she arranged the hyacinths in the vase. "Considering that you didn't seem to care . . ." Megan hesitated. By way of a side glance, Megan was able to see that Carl's mood had not done a one-hundred-and-eighty-degree jump on her. "They're very pretty," she safely concluded.

The couple shared the kitchen chores as they had the previous evening. Conversation was a bit different in that it seemed to center on Rio de Janeiro and São Paulo, even though he admitted that the cities didn't interest him very much.

"The cities seemed contaminated by Italian,

German, and Japanese influences. I wanted to be in the heart of the rain forest."

"Had you been to Europe or the Far East?"

"Never got to the Far East, though I'd like to someday. I grew up in Europe."

"Really!" Megan turned to Carl and dropped the head of lettuce she had been pulling apart. She saw Carl's face freeze. He looked at the lettuce, then at her. *Come on, Carl, it's only lettuce,* she silently protested. He must have seen the silent plea on her face, because he started to laugh.

"Doesn't take much to impress you."

Megan chuckled, too. She bent and scooped the lettuce from the floor. "My father was in the armed services, so we moved around a lot, but for some reason he never was stationed outside the States." There was a pause. She waited for him to explain why he grew up in Europe.

"You were asking about Tupi earthenware before."

Her eyes fluttered. Tupi earthenware? "Oh, yes, when we were coming up the path."

Carl nodded. "I have one in the study on top of the bookcase."

"I hadn't noticed it before. May I go get it?"

Carl nodded with a smile.

Megan again dropped the lettuce, but this time into a bowl; then she rushed from the kitchen to the study. As she entered the room, she spotted an earthenware pot centered on the top ledge of the bookcase.

When she tried to reach for it, she discovered she was a tad too short. She positioned a straight-backed chair in front of the bookcase. The chair's seat consisted of old caning, and Megan was not sure it would support her weight. Not wanting to call Carl, she climbed up anyway. For once she was lucky; it held through her mission. While carrying the pot the short distance to the kitchen, Megan noted the red and black tracery edged on the outer white coating.

"Careful, Megan."

One would have assumed she took the warning as a challenge, because she immediately stumbled over her own feet, righting herself at the last minute. She grinned apologetically before placing the earthenware on the table.

"What a pretty trim," she said, fingering the red and black trail circling the pot.

"The tracery is meant to be a maze. It's supposed to confuse the evil spirits searching for the human remains inside the earthenware."

Megan peeked inside the pot.

"At least that's what the folklore is. There's nothing inside of it right now."

She was relieved; after all, she had touched it, carried it close to her body. Of course, it was still kind of creepy to think that someone's remains were once inside it. She wiped the palms of her hands on her jeans.

"The food's almost ready. Why don't you clear the table?"

Clear the table. His voice echoed inside her head. Knowing that she didn't want to touch the pot again, Megan suggested that she should finish the salad first. If she was slow enough, Carl would set the table himself.

Megan was partly right. Carl lifted the pot, but only to hand it to Megan.

"Please return it."

Megan gulped. "Why don't I set the table? You know exactly where you want that placed."

"Don't tell me you're afraid of this pot."

Her nose wrinkled as she worried her bottom lip. "I hadn't realized that people's remains were put into the earthenware. I guess I hadn't gotten far enough into the journal to learn that piece of information."

"Actually, I don't remember writing about that. It was just a fact that I stored away inside my head." Carl looked at the earthenware with admiration. "A pretty place to spend eternity, don't you think?"

"I'm claustrophobic, so it has no appeal for me."

"There's no more room inside a coffin, you know. Here at least you don't have the earth pressing down on you. The pot can be left open to the sky, unlike a coffin, which is fastened shut."

"Didn't you say dinner was done?"

Carl smiled and presented the earthenware to her.

"It's difficult for me to reach the top of the

bookcase. I had to use the cane chair to get up there, and I'm not sure I could do it again without disastrous results."

"You should make peace with death, Megan."

"Have you?"

"I believe I've come to a compromise with it today."

"In what way?"

Carl looked sharply at Megan. "I'll return the earthenware to the study. Set the table."

Megan took a deep breath, then released a soft sigh. In many ways, Carl was an enigma; yet she felt drawn to him even during his dark moods.

By the time Carl returned to the kitchen, the table had been set and Megan was dividing up the food.

"What took you so long?"

"Did you miss me?" he asked, resting his hands upon her small hips and leaning into the hollow between her shoulder blades.

The seductive Carl was back. Maybe he had multiple personalities, she thought.

"Careful, or we'll both get burned," she said while resting a pot down on an iron trivet.

Carl pulled back. "Bring the journal to the table, and I'll discuss some of the passages with you," he said, moving across the room to take his place at the dinner table.

Chapter 20
The Last Journal

The chit was charming at dinner with all her questions and oohing and aahing. Carl was getting used to her tendency to snoop. Her awkwardness was becoming almost alluring, but then, his contact with Beverly that day had made everything seem a bit more bearable. No longer did Carl believe that Beverly would somehow foil the incantation he had worked over her, although for some reason she did appear to be decaying at a faster rate than her predecessors. Still, his body was gaining strength from hers; that was what was important.

He remembered seeing Beverly's frame against the soiled mattress, the scrawny limbs and bloated trunk. Carl made note that he would have to bring in a new mattress, since her body had spilled its fluids on various portions of the current one. She may not be dying neatly, but she was amenable. He had turned to thank her before passing through the French doors, but when he spoke she had not responded, choosing to lie quietly with eyes shut. Had she heard?

With a call of "Good night," Megan brought Carl out of his reverie.

Megan was using the bed and he the bumpy couch, but he hadn't wanted to push her. She was skittish every time he was close to her, and she practically stopped breathing if he touched her. He knew with time she would come around, and now he was confident that he had that. His former paramour was cooperating. Hadn't Beverly seduced him that afternoon? There was a minor, weak protest from her in the midst of their lovemaking, but she succumbed once he was settled inside her.

Carl removed the key from his pocket and opened the bottom desk drawer. He pulled out the sketch pad, flipped through the pages until he came upon Megan's profile. What could he add or subtract? He tried to visualize Megan; then he quickly sketched out a frontal view, but it wasn't Megan. It was Beverly, with the hollowed-out eyes, the flattened cartilage across the bridge of her nose, and the bloated cheeks, which were now slowly sinking into her cheekbones. Carl scratched out the face, shut the pad, and threw it back into the drawer. After kicking the drawer closed with his foot, Carl locked it.

There was time. He would finish Megan's drawing before she left. Carl was sure of it.

Megan had played the Grand Inquisitor that night, trying to find out why he had traveled to the Amazon. Carl had told her the truth: He had wanted to do this before he died. What he hadn't told her was that he had been about to die. Except for luck and a very wise headman, by now he would have been buried as deep as the drawings in his yard.

He stood, exited the study, and went to the hall closet, where his Nikon sat on the top shelf. *Tomorrow I should take a photograph of Megan for my album,* he thought as he took the camera down. Suddenly he remembered another chore he had set for himself.

Leaving the camera on the kitchen table as he passed through, he headed for the back door. Not wanting to disturb Megan, he softly stepped down the back steps of the porch, hating each creak. He glanced to the side of the house to make sure no light came from the bedroom; then he checked the back door, which was open. All there was to see was the brown tile floor and a hint of illumination shining into the kitchen from the bulb in the hallway.

Four steps to his left, he squatted down to pull out a block of wood, behind which was the last journal. The back cover was smeared with dirt, and the front seemed to have been stuck into some giant spider's web. He brushed the silken threads off, then blew across the back cover. For such an important book, it was badly damaged. Pages were loose, ink stains abounded on the edges, and the binding was starting to come apart. It didn't matter, because Carl had the significant sections of the journal memorized. Hadn't he used the spell at least two dozen times?

Carl walked over to the old shed, placed the book on the ground, and removed the door from its hinges. Once he retrieved the book, Carl entered the shed. By moonglow he hid the journal behind a shovel and between two boxes full of film negatives. He threw an old rag casually on top of the pile.

After covering his tracks, Carl returned to the kitchen, switching the light on as he entered. He checked the film and battery in the camera. He had been a photojournalist, and he still had all the equipment to process and develop his own work. No one would have to know of the girl's visit.

If it hadn't been for the rare fungus disease he had contracted in the Caribbean, he would still be working professionally. However, he did not dare expose himself to any publicity, because there were people who probably assumed he was dead by now, and he couldn't explain to them why he wasn't. Instead, he satisfied himself with capturing the environs on film, as banal as they were.

Carl smiled, thinking about how excited Megan would probably be when he suggested the photo shoot. Maybe he could get her to disrobe; that always made his task easier, although he had been able to achieve that with only a handful of the women. However, Megan was younger and apt to be less uptight than the rest.

He left the camera on the table and clicked off the kitchen light. In the bathroom, Carl undressed; as he did, he checked muscle tone, hair growth, nails, color and elasticity of skin. No deterioration was noticeable; indeed, his body seemed to be firming up more each day as Beverly wilted away. This was the strongest reaction his body had ever had to the strange power that he had acquired.

While dreading to sleep on the uncomfortable couch, Carl promised himself that it would be for only one or two more nights; then he would be back in his own bed next to the youthful, budding woman with full breasts, a tiny waist that spread into tightly molded hips, above slinky, long legs. However, that night he dreamed of Beverly.

Chapter 21
I Never Want to Hurt You

Summer's breath swept across Carl's body. He turned his head to the open French doors and watched as the sun spun shadows through the doorway. The reflection of a tree branch sagged as a bird landed, flicking its wings to steady itself. Leaves spiraled into sharp-edged designs against the simple white wall. The ceiling fan was still, allowing nature the freedom to warble, chirp, and rustle.

He never had been so peaceful. Between his legs he could feel Beverly's white nylon stocking. The lacy elastic that banded the top of her hose prickled his skin, arousing him. Her brown, lush hair lay atop his biceps. His left hand reached across his body to touch the silkiness of her locks. Bev-

*erly responded by nuzzling her face against his
breast. She lightly touched her tongue to his nipple, leaving a spot of saliva, which sent sensuous
shivers through his body. Her fingers weaved
through the bristly, dark blond hair covering his
pubis.*

*Carl breathed deeply. There was only the scent
of her sex. It smote the air and embedded the
sheets, staining the material with the memory of
their passion. The white nylon slid across his
shin, reaching down to his toes. Beverly's body
stiffened against his. Her moans and gyrations
signaled her need. She squirmed about until her
body covered his. Carl grabbed her arms when she
started to rise upon his hips. He liked the contact
of the two bodies and didn't want it to end so
soon. Her hair covered her features, but he knew
she understood when her breasts sagged back
down upon his chest. He whispered her name
into strands of her hair. In answer, Beverly nib-
bled and licked at his throat.*

*Finally, he pushed her up to a seated position.
That was when he saw the marks he had made
on her arms. Bluish-black rings circled the flesh
above the elbows. It was where he had held her.*

"Beverly, I'm sorry."

*She flung back her head, carrying waves of hair
back and off her face. She looked at the bruises
and smiled.*

*"It's all right, Carl. They won't last forever," she
promised.*

Beverly passed her index finger across his lips,

and he reached up to do the same on hers. As his finger moved, the skin underneath began to crack, leaving a caky surface for him to kiss, which he did when she bent forward. Fetid saliva passed from her to him. Quickly, Carl turned his head to spit out the foamy juice.

When he moved his head back to her, she was seated upon his manhood. Beverly lifted one of his hands to her mouth. She lapped and sucked his fingertips. Almost imperceptibly, her body moved, her hips a metronome for their desire.

His free hand gripped her waist. Guiding her to his own beat, he shut his eyes and listened to her soft panting and felt the rib cage above his grasp expand and contract. He perceived her struggle for air. He opened his eyes to look at her. Beverly's mouth was wide, and he could hear the rales rattling inside her chest.

"Beverly, are you all right?"

Letting go of his hand, she reached down and caressed his jaw.

"I love you," she whispered.

As she stroked his face, his grip on her waist tightened. Beverly winced as if in pain, but she did not pull away or slow the pace they both were keeping. Instead, they moved toward their peaks, until Carl pulled Beverly's head down to his mouth, where he bit her lips, taking in her blood as he spilled his own liquid.

Done, their bodies separated. Carl felt the mattress sag next to him. He rolled to his side toward her. Crisscrossing one side of her waist were broad welts.

"Did I do that?"

"Why are you surprised?"

"I never want to hurt you," he said, dipping down to kiss the irritated skin.

Her hand skimmed his right shoulder blade.

"I know that," she assured him.

Carl stretched back onto his side of the bed, resting his head on the goose-down pillow, and slept next to his love.

Chapter 22
Prowler

When Carl woke the next morning, he felt refreshed. He might not even have noticed the pain in his back immediately, except for the fact that when he rose a spring broke the material of the couch right where the lower half of his spine had been.

"Damn," he muttered, rubbing the sore, red skin.

A pot dropped to the floor in the kitchen, and Carl called out Beverly's name.

Silence.

What was he doing? Beverly never came here; she couldn't be here. Instead, she'd be waiting down the river for him. He must have fallen asleep on the couch after reading. He looked around the floor near where he stood, but saw no book or magazine.

A slight clink from the kitchen whispered into the living room. Someone had to be in the next room. Naked, Carl moved to the bathroom, where he found his jeans lying across the rim of the bathtub. Swiftly he pulled the jeans up over his hips, not bothering to fasten them before going to the study to get his Beretta. Carrying the gun behind his back, Carl moved down the hallway toward the kitchen. He heard the steady clink of a spoon inside a glass. Who the hell would make themselves breakfast in a stranger's house? he wondered. Carl recalled making love with Beverly and staying the night with her. So how did he get here?

Once he saw Megan moon him from under one of his shirts, as she bent over to remove a tray from the oven, he knew he had been dreaming. Yes, he had made love to Beverly the day before, but not the Beverly he had so clearly visualized in his dream. That Beverly was the one he knew before he had buried her drawing.

By the time he had reoriented himself, the empty pan Megan had been holding had clattered to the ground and she herself was standing in front of the stove with a mouth opened so wide and round that she looked like an old voodoo doll he had seen used in Haiti. What was wrong with the girl? he wondered as he followed her stare down to the gun dangling loosely between the fingers of his left hand.

"Sorry, Megan. I woke with a start, and, actually, I didn't remember you were here. I'll put it away." Megan appeared to be in a stupor. "You're making breakfast, I see. Anything special?" Megan's lips closed tightly, and Carl could almost hear her gulp down the air that had been captured inside her mouth. "Are those muffins on the counter behind you? Megan? Megan?" Intrepid she was not, he decided.

"Didn't mean to drop the pan. It just slipped."

"I'm not going to shoot you for dropping a pan. The Tupi earthenware, maybe. Megan, at least smile. I thought you were an intruder, and I probably wouldn't even shoot you if you dropped the earthenware."

Finally he saw a smile brighten the gaunt face.

"I guess we were both startled. Oh, yes, they're corn muffins. I wanted to surprise you with a big breakfast. Surprise," she said, bouncing in place. Carl watched her red curls spring into the air like golden rusted coils that bounced back onto her forehead and cheeks. He always knew that he didn't have the patience for dealing with children, although many women had tried to tell him otherwise.

"I'll return this to the study," he said, bringing forth the gun. He caught sight of a slight backward motion of Megan's bare feet. "Have you ever used a gun?"

She shook her head.

As Carl turned to leave, Megan called out to him.

"Carl, where do you keep the gun?"

"Why?"

"Maybe I should also know where it is in case of burglars, rapists, or murderers."

"They're rare around here."

"Then why did you think I was one?"

"There's always the exception. I wasn't quite as dramatic as you. I only assumed there was an intruder, perhaps a kid or a tramp. Who else would rob me of my pots and pans?"

"Well, if that's all you thought, don't you think you were a bit overarmed?"

"There's always the exception, Megan, always the exception."

Carl was beginning to feel weary, and it wasn't past nine in the morning yet.

Through breakfast, Megan chuckled about how silly the morning's escapade had been. Carl was interested in bedding and drawing the girl again; he didn't know how much longer he could take her drivel. He had been intrigued by her naïveté initially, but not now. Beverly had been a much more literate and worldly conversationalist. Carl caught himself on that thought; he had to stop comparing the two. One was lost to him as a companion, and the other would be leaving shortly, and before she did he had to have captured her precise image.

"I'm going to work in my study today. I hope you don't mind entertaining yourself."

"Maybe this idea of my staying isn't—"

Carl leaped to a standing position.

"Please, Megan. I'll be alone through most of

the winter. Won't you stay at least for the summer, so I'll have some memories of human company?"

"Not the summer, Carl, I told you."

"I'm sorry. Stay the two weeks, please."

"But you seem so busy."

"I do work for a living and have to finish a special project, but I promise to make some time for you. Matter of fact, I could skip today and we could—"

"No, I can wander around on my own for a while."

He watched the young woman shake her head while tapping her short fingernails against the oak table.

"Perhaps we could go into town tomorrow?" she asked.

Town! She would drive him crazy.

"Better still, we'll picnic."

"The garden where your rental is." Megan brightened with this thought while Carl sagged back down into his chair.

"Maybe, but there are scenic places more local."

"Well, the garden must need care, and we could—"

"I took care of things yesterday. Remember? I stopped off there instead of going to town."

He saw her glance over at the vase full of hyacinths.

"Has my journal bored you already?"

"No, but I would like to spend more time with you."

"Does it matter where?"

Megan didn't answer right away.

"It shouldn't," she said without conviction.

Carl thought briefly about taking Megan into town and passing her off as a niece, but he decided that would be too dangerous. Then he thought of the camera, which had been shoved to the side of the table.

"We could take photographs later today, if you'd like."

"I'm a terrible photographer. When I'm lucky enough to get the film in correctly, I always seem to chop off heads and limbs."

"I'd like you to model for me."

"Are you professional? Is that what you do for a living?"

Carl hesitated. "Semiprofessional. I do it for my own interest now."

"Were you a professional?"

Doubting that Megan would have heard of him, he admitted to his former line of work.

"That's why you traveled so much."

"Partly. What if we make a date, say, for three o'clock?"

"That's fine. I found the journal on the counter this morning; maybe I'll read outdoors until then."

Carl rose and gave Megan a paternal kiss on the forehead, then retreated inside his study. He could hear her clearing the table and running the water while he locked the door.

He sat at the desk and waited for silence.

When the front door slammed, Carl knew he had the house to himself. He went through the necessary ritual to retrieve the sketch pad. Then spreading the pad open, he leaned forward to see how much he had accomplished. Megan's facial features still needed some work. A few of Beverly's lines had crept onto Megan's forehead.

I have to block Beverly out of my mind before this waif decides to take off, he contemplated. Perhaps he should work harder at making the girl's life happy here. The last thing he wanted was her departure before he finished her double on paper.

Many times Carl attempted the girl's pixie face. Half the time he had to erase a wrinkle out of place on the forehead, a dimple in the left cheek, hair that was sketched too darkly. He threw down the pencil. Would another visit to Beverly help, or would it cloud his mind even more? What had Beverly done to him?

While lifting the pencil again, Carl turned to a clean sheet, renewing his effort. He would stay at his desk for most of the day, bypassing lunch and the three o'clock appointment with Megan.

Chapter 23
Megan and Beverly

Megan flittered down the porch steps with Carl's first journal clasped in her left hand, her step so light that she barely touched the slatted wooden boards. She had every intention of returning to the area from which the hyacinth fragrance emanated, but by the time she arrived at the turnoff, she had changed her mind. Too full of energy to sleep, Megan had risen early—a mistake, she later had decided when Carl surprised her, weapon in hand. Still, even that episode had invigorated her with adrenaline. No, there was no way she could sit for hours and read by herself.

When she was a girl, she had taken turns with her father rowing when they went out to the middle of the lake to fish. Megan would borrow Carl's rowboat and go down the river to the real hyacinth garden. She paused only for a second, knowing that she should ask Carl's permission, but earlier she had heard the lock on his den door click into place. The man definitely wanted no disturbances; besides, she would return before three and he wouldn't even know where she had spent the morning.

Megan's pace quickened to a jog. She was delighted that her injured knee was more flexible and that she could keep busy and not impose herself on her host. A little out of breath, Megan halted in front of the boat and looked around for a clean place on which to lay the journal while she flipped the boat over and hauled it into the water. Finally, she decided on a small, barren boulder, which had somehow escaped the dewy green moss that seemed to cover everything else in the vicinity.

Once the boat was afloat, Megan hopped in and began rowing, forgetting the journal. In the pleasant breeze, she shook out her curls and stretched her arms forward as far as she could reach. Daddy had always said that the best part of their fishing expeditions was when Megan guided their small boat home, and he could lean back, inhaling the rank smell of the fish, an odor that always made her mother pinch her nose. Mother never went with them. Megan and her father silently appreciated that, because their time together was precious, since he would often have to go off on special duty for a week or two. She closed her eyes, and her memory called up visions of childhood expeditions.

A teardrop squeezed through Megan's shut eyes. When they opened, the tear fell down onto her jeans. Megan was distracted from her family reverie when she saw the yellow house blocking the view between the trees. She made her way inland and dragged the boat onto shore, leaving it lying lopsided, spilling its puddle on the roots of tall grass.

Her walk up to the garden was sluggish, since Megan was a bit out of breath from the rowing and hauling. The house didn't look any different than it had the first time she had seen it. Vines still crept up the porch steps, and the slats of the jalousie still had the incredible ability to move when they shouldn't. *Must be the way the sun hits them*, she thought.

Megan was tempted to peek into the house. Did Carl leave it unlocked? she wondered. Considering how paranoid he seemed to be that morning, she doubted it. On the porch, the white wicker furniture clustered in a circle as if conferring about this intruder. They could be old women gossiping about the outrageous behavior of today's youth, Megan thought. Each chair had a floral cushion snugly placed in the seat. The table was bare, except for a colorful butterfly that had just landed on its center. Lemonade, that's what was missing, Megan decided. Some cold lemonade to pass the approaching hot afternoon in comfort.

She climbed the steps and pulled one of the

chairs out so that she could sit. Her chair was in front of the jalousie, and from where she sat she could almost see the river through the trees. Megan wondered why Carl had decided not to live here. The view was better, there was a lovely garden, and even the unkempt front lawn was far more lush than the area surrounding his home. But she hadn't seen the inside of this house yet, and perhaps therein was the reason, although she couldn't imagine anything drearier than the faded rugs and ancient, tired furniture in Carl's house. This house seemed brighter, cheerier than the drab blue one she had left.

Megan's shoulders shivered in the heat of the morning sun. Might she be coming down with a cold? she wondered. Not that she felt chilly or ill; she felt peculiar, like . . . like . . .

"Plain and simple, Megan, you are trespassing," she said out loud. "Guilty," she muttered, then set out for the garden in the back of the house.

The garden gate had been left open, and Megan ambled in as if it were her private retreat. The French doors were closed, the curtains drawn, as they had been the last time she had been there. Hyacinth perfume tickled her senses, making her feel giddy, but she saddened when she saw how uncared for the garden was.

"Right, Carl, you took care of the flowers when you were here yesterday." That man had no green thumb, not even a pale imitation of one.

"I wonder if there aren't some garden supplies around here, so I could spruce you guys up," she said to the cluster of hyacinths and roses.

Megan turned and was startled to see that the French doors were wide open. A dark figure loomed in the center of the doorway. There was a husky, wheezing sound, but Megan could not make out any words.

"I'm sorry I intruded." *What am I saying,* she thought, *this is Carl's house, and he told me no one was here.* "I don't think you belong here," she said in a shaky voice. "This property belongs to a friend of mine, and, believe me, he takes ownership very seriously."

"Does he own you?" the figure managed to rasp out.

Megan tried to decide whether this thing was human. At length, she figured it might be. She proceeded to the next step: decoding which sex it was. The robe was black velvet. A shiny line seemed to drip down the front collar; Megan couldn't tell whether it was a fresh stain or some substance that had dried with a sheen. A dark woolen shawl was pulled over its head, the edges of the covering resting across the thing's small shoulders. The figure's feet were fitted into leather boots, the toes of which protruded incongruously from under the soft robe.

"Do you need a home? You can't really stay here, but maybe I could help you. Do you have any family?"

"Carl."

"Are you related to Carl?" Megan was confused. "He said the house was empty."

"Carl lies."

Megan watched the figure draw one of its hands out of a pocket. The hand was gloved in leather and beckoned Megan forward.

She gulped and asked whether the figure wanted her to get Carl. The hand quickly shook a negative response.

"Come closer, girl, I cannot speak loudly. It strains my vocal chords."

With a sigh, Megan inched forward. As she did, she noticed that the air clouded with a stink that had to be issuing from the body before her. Megan sniffed a bit, then reasoned that this person had not bathed in some time, if ever. She had done some work at a homeless shelter, but this went beyond anything she could remember. It wasn't dirt; it was more like decay. Trying to overcome her aversion, Megan stopped an arm's length away from the figure.

"You're frightened of me. I'm not the one who's planning to hurt you. No, you sleep with him, slut."

Megan stepped back. The figure wavered and shook as if it were about to go poof and disappear before Megan's eyes, but it didn't. Slowly, it returned to its former placid, stiff position.

"I'm sorry, child, but he comes so rarely now, and I miss him."

The figure was whining and pawing the floor

with the soles of its black leather boots.

"Is he your son?"

"My . . ." The figure nodded almost reluctantly, thought Megan.

"Are you ill?" Megan realized how stupid the question was after she asked it. The figure obviously smelled of disease.

The figure shook its head in denial.

"Past ill, girl. I'm beyond hope."

"What's your name?" Megan moved closer, holding her breath occasionally so that her breakfast would not rise up in protest.

"I was Beverly."

Carl must have wanted to keep her a secret because of her health. She did seem delicate. How could she bear all that clothing?

"I'm Megan. I was hiking and ran into your son a few days ago down by the river. He must have just finished visiting. Come to think of it, I hope I didn't disturb the both of you." Megan remembered the movement at the jalousie. "Perhaps you remember seeing me." Beverly gave no sign of recognition. "I had hurt my knee earlier in the day, then clumsily tripped over your son's boat." Beverly's body stiffened. "Carl invited me back to his home so I could take care of the wound. He asked me to stay awhile to keep him company, but today he's working and I'm on my own."

Megan had been talking slowly, precisely, and a little more loudly than normal.

"Do you like the garden?"

Megan enthusiastically praised the stunning flora. This pleased Beverly, who invited Megan into the house.

"Gosh. I don't want to disturb you."

"There's an enclosed porch at the other side of the house with all sorts of gardening tools, even some fertilizer. I'd like you to care for the garden, since I no longer can. Please." Beverly moved to the right, turned sideways, and extended a gloved hand in invitation.

This was like tripping over Dracula's lair in the midst of the forest, thought Megan. If the woman smelled bad from here, what could the house be like?

"I'm sure Carl would prefer to take care of the landscape himself; after all, he is planning on renting the house." Megan bit her tongue. "I mean, he has some sort of plans for the house." She knew there was no way out.

"Yes, he has plans, but not just for the house. Maybe I'll share them with you one day."

"Listen, I have to get back. Carl and I are going to take photographs this afternoon."

"Really! But he likes to sketch."

"Sketch?" Megan decided that the old woman must be a bit senile, confusing her son's interests with the hyacinth woman's. It dawned on Megan that this woman could fill in many of the blank spaces. What was the hyacinth woman like? How hard had Carl taken the breakup? The questions were probably too personal for his mother to answer right now, but if she continued to visit and helped in the garden . . . Megan peered past the woman into the shadows of the bedroom.

"You say the tools are on the enclosed porch? Is that near the bedroom?"

"I'll show you where they are, or better, would you like me to bring them to you?"

Megan looked at the old woman. Somehow she didn't look strong enough to carry a garden spade. *So why be afraid, Megan? Hold your nose and make a dash for the equipment.*

"Would it be easier if I came around the front?"

"Either you carry them through the house or around it, child."

Around somehow sounded safer and allowed for more fresh air.

"I'll meet you at the front door, if you don't mind."

The woman emitted a cackle, which took Megan back to her childhood days of witches and Halloween.

"It's not me you should be afraid of. Do you feel safe in Carl's house? Do you touch him and feel the hellish fire in him? Do you cling to the fiend's sour flesh and believe he loves you? When his seed spills down your thighs, does it ever burn like acid?"

"Maybe today is not a good gardening day, ma'am. I'm sorry if I disturbed you." She turned to go.

"Megan," the crone called. "I have something important to tell you."

173

Megan hesitated.

"It's about Carl. He's sick, but he won't let anyone help him. Perhaps you could cure him."

She faced the woman again. "I'm not a doctor or a nurse or anything like that. I was barely able to dress my skinned knee."

"Give me some time, Megan, please. I'll think of a way to . . . to help. Meet me at the front door. The spade, hoe, and gloves will be on the porch when you get there. You like the garden, and it, too, will die without your help."

It, too? What did this woman mean? Megan wondered. Was Carl so ill that his life was in danger? Megan remembered how resolutely her father had met death. Why couldn't he have let his daughter save him from the solitude?

"Do you have pruning shears?" Megan asked.

"Of course. Meet me at the front door."

For most of the day, Megan worked silently in the garden, while Beverly leaned against the frame of the French door, chortling once in a while asthmatically, until Megan noticed that it was almost three o'clock. Hurriedly Megan pulled all her supplies together and left the bundle on the garden swing.

"I'll be back tomorrow, the next day at the latest."

"Oh, Megan, don't mention that you spoke to me. Carl, well . . . he thinks I frighten people. We know better, don't we?" Beverly let out a low, strident cackle, and Megan grudgingly agreed while sprinting out of the garden.

Chapter 24
The Photo Shoot

Carl was sweeping bits of eraser off of his nearly perfect profile of Megan when he heard the front door bang. His watch, which rested on the windowsill, read four o'clock. Thinking Megan would be furious, Carl speedily hid his work before unlocking the door.

"I'm sorry, Carl. I got caught up in what I was doing, and I forgot our date. If you give me five minutes to throw some water on my face and tidy up my hair, as tidy as I can get it, I'll be right with you." Her voice got dimmer the farther she strode from him toward the bedroom.

He scratched his head and smirked at his luck.

"Take your time," he said generously. "I'll make sure the camera is ready."

While in the kitchen, Carl cut himself some

Edam cheese and fetched a few crackers out of a tin he kept in the back of the cupboard.

"What a good idea," Megan said as she entered the room and eyed the snack Carl had set before himself. Carl tossed her an apple from the fruit bowl, then offered her a slice of the cheese.

"How far did you get in the journal today?"

Megan shrugged.

"Weren't you reading?"

"Not all day."

Carl heard the apple crunch against her teeth.

"Okay, part of the day you read. What did you do with the other part?"

"Wandered around."

"Where?" Carl's voice became hard. His hand dropped a cheese-covered cracker back onto a dish.

"Here and there."

"Mostly where, Megan?"

"Down by the river."

Relieved, Carl continued to finish his snack.

"Does that mean you spent most of the day lazily dipping your feet in the river and seeing how far you could throw stones?"

"You know me very well." Her smile displayed an impish guilt.

"Reading my journal is not a school assignment, Megan. If you're bored with the—"

"Not bored, too full of energy to sit still and concentrate."

"Think you'll be able to sit still for me?" he

asked, reaching across the counter to lift his camera.

Megan fluffed up her hair, straightened the collar on her denim shirt, rubbed her index finger across her front teeth, and smiled brilliantly.

"Perfect." Carl snapped several shots.

"Denim looks very nice on you, Megan, but what we need is a little hint of femininity. Perhaps some lace or ribbons."

"Got it." Megan scurried into the bedroom, and Carl followed. She looked surprised when, after rummaging in her backpack, she turned around and saw Carl in the doorway. She had a lacy camisole dangling from her fingertips.

"Good contrast." Carl was disappointed when Megan rushed into the bathroom, calling back that she would only be a minute. He tapped his callused fingers against the camera as he walked to the wicker chair, where he allowed his body to collapse onto the threadbare cushion.

Megan reappeared with just a snippet of the lace showing at the top of her denim shirt. He snapped another picture.

"A few more buttons and show some shoulder."

"What kind of photography did you do, anyway?"

"I was a photojournalist. Took pictures of things I was writing about: cities, towns, royalty, homes, women."

"I can guess which was your favorite."

Carl laughed. "And you, too, know me well." Carl saw the blend of ego and fascination in her eyes. Here was a girl who hadn't yet been allowed to explore her sexuality. Not a virgin, but not sure of her powers. He watched as she surreptitiously pulled on the sleeve of her shirt, revealing a white shoulder. He snapped another photo.

Aggressively, Carl walked over to Megan, unbuttoned the denim shirt, grabbed the collar, and pulled off the shirt without any reprimand from Megan. The lace of the camisole clung to the mold of her breasts. Each nipple darkened the center of a sheer swirl in the material. Carl undid the button and zipper of her jeans. Megan's hands reflexively rose to her hips, barely touching the material.

"Sit on the bed; the lighting and background are better. Snapping pictures of you in front of the bathroom doesn't quite do it."

Without untying the laces, Megan slipped off her sneakers. She folded one foot beneath her as she sat down on the coverlet. Carl watched as she pulled her shoulders back and gave a pretty pout for the camera. Yes, she was enjoying the attention. It was a chance for her to experiment with her sensuality.

"Turn sideways and throw your head back."

She followed directions very well.

"Have you photographed a lot of beautiful women?"

178

"I've photographed a lot of women with a wide range of charms."

Megan looked at Carl and squinted. "What range do I fall into?"

"A bit more skin, and I could tell you for sure."

She smiled and bowed her head, allowing her red curls to fall over her cheeks and forehead. Slowly she drew her hands up her thighs to the waistband of her jeans, then with an exaggerated wiggle she slipped the jeans down her hips until at last the jeans fell to the floor. While throwing her head back, Megan reached her right hand up and drew her fingers through her hair. When she rose onto her knees, Carl could see that she wore a tiny thong that hardly covered anything in front, and in the back it seemed to emphasize her firm, spreading buttocks.

Carl kept taking shots, although his slim linen trousers felt weighted by his growing desire. He knew that Megan was not performing for the camera. She was testing her ability to snare this older man with her charms, and she was succeeding. However, before he could seduce the seducer, he had to have several nude shots in order to complete the drawing.

"Push the straps down from your shoulders."

Obediently, the girl complied. Her nipples were pointed and hard, her breathing rapid and shallow.

"Don't tease the camera, Megan. Take that damn camisole off."

"Are you sure it's the camera I'm teasing?"

"Can't you see the smoke coming out the back?"

Megan glanced down at his crotch. Obviously, she knew what she was stimulating. She nonchalantly lifted off the camisole and dropped it over the side of the bed.

"You can do better than that, sweetie."

Megan stuck out her tongue and licked every one of her fingers, then with digits spread wide she slid her nails under the thong's band, stretching the material as she deliberately eased the silken panties down over her skin.

When the discarded garment settled on the lens of the Nikon, Carl almost lost control. Rubbing the silk between his thumb and index finger, Carl lifted the material from the lens and raised it to his lips, then dropped the garment and furiously started snapping the writhing, wriggling Megan.

Carl advanced slowly on his subject, the click of the shutter the only sound to be heard above their thick breathing. Tentatively he reached out a hand, touching one of her firm breasts. He pushed his hand forward until he could feel the dense, tender teat. Megan had not brushed away his hand or cringed from the calluses he knew crusted his large palms. This picture-taking session had been as titillating for her as it had been for him. One goal was complete. Could he push for the bonus points? Carl watched Megan through the viewfinder. Her hands were searching her own body, skimming across the most sensitive areas as if the heat burned her fingertips.

With one hand Carl carefully laid the camera on the rug at the foot of the bed, while retaining his hold on the extended tip of Megan's breast. His hand slid from her breast, trailing the girl's hand downward. Both hands halted for a moment, Megan's small hand hovering over Carl's, until he gradually meted out a rhythm for her passion. Her hand settled upon his in harmony with his circular motion, her taut hips raised to gain the full vibration of his beat.

Carl's free hand began unbuttoning his shirt and fly. Afraid to break the metered touch that hypnotized the girl, Carl pulled his trousers down with one hand just enough to free his tumescence. Once he had slipped two of his fingers inside her, he knew she would not reject him. She was flooded with the thick, inviting fluid of her womanhood. He raised his body over Megan's and easily entered her. She squeezed her arms tightly around his middle as she bucked fiercely and cried out her panting breaths. Soon they each erupted in their own release, without the comfort of a spiritual union.

Megan held on to Carl long after his desire had diminished. He escaped in his mind to the delights he would find on film, the delights that would unblock the barrier preventing him from completing the drawing of Megan.

He heard her whimper softly into his shoulder and instinctively brushed her hair back from her face, kissing the pert nose he had managed to duplicate so perfectly that day. A girl forging her way into womanhood, into death, he thought. A pang of regret almost filtered through his armor, but he didn't love the girl. She was sensuous, a good bed partner, that was all. Still, he knew he was stealing something precious from someone who would never be able to identify the thief.

She eased her hold on his body. His ribs ached from the vehemence of her hug. Her lips touched his collarbone, his neck, his chin; she was searching for his mouth when he pulled away.

"Perhaps I'll no longer have to sleep on that seedy couch of mine?" he asked with a raised eyebrow.

At first Megan looked confused. Her eyes focused on his before she answered. "It's been silly. Why shouldn't I share the bed with you?"

Carl could hear the unhappiness in her nonchalant reply. He might still need her if something had gone wrong with the film, so he relented and kissed Megan on the lips, allowing her tongue to brush against his in an imitation of love.

Chapter 25
Father

That night Megan lay with eyes open and breath hushed in order not to awaken the sleeping body next to her. Prior to retiring they had made love, or fornicated, depending on each lover's viewpoint. Carl didn't love Megan; she sensed that when she groped for his mouth or when she whispered his name and received no response other than the lumping of his lips. Yet he needed this connection with her, not from pure animal instinct, she concluded, but to retain his hold on life. His mother had told her that he was ill, a life-threatening disease—something he had never bothered to reveal to Megan. Why had she permitted this sexual encounter without protection? What if she were pregnant—or worse, caught the same disease he had?

Megan raised her hands to her face and sobbed. She rubbed the palms deep into her eyelids, trying to press away the tension behind them.

Carl rolled onto his back. Megan stopped breathing, but he was not awake, apparently only dreaming as he muttered unrecognizable words in a slow, sleepy drawl. Megan lowered her hands to cover her mouth, stifling the little cries that wanted to issue forth. In the morning, she would ask him about his health. No! She would tell him she knew he was sick and wanted to know what disease he had.

She glanced over at Carl. He looked so healthy in the dimness of the moonlight. Hell, he looked healthy under the starkness of daylight. What could be wrong with him? *Oh, great, Megan, you're worried what might be wrong with him when you should be figuring out why your head's so screwed up that you've taken no precautions to protect yourself.*

Megan rolled to her side to face Carl. Maybe she should wake him and confront him with what she knew. *Right, and maybe you would start raving like a lunatic, about how he should have made sure he had a condom, and what if you're pregnant, and on and on. It's your own carelessness, Megan, not his.*

With a light touch Megan reached out and drew back a few strands of golden-white hair that lay upon his temple. He appeared so strong, but so had her father until the final weeks before he died, and he hadn't told her about his illness either. The last few years of his life Megan had taken her father for granted. He would always be there after she was finished with the football games, the basketball games, the parties, the outings, the summer camps, but Megan was never there for him. Not there when he first learned of his cancer, not there when he was struggling through his therapy. She hadn't even paid any attention to the progressive loss of weight, the hardy complexion turning sallow. She never asked questions and was told nothing until the hospitalization, but then it was too late. Her father quickly fell into a coma, and it was impossible to make up for the times when she had ignored him. All she could do was sit by the bed and talk to the fragile husk that once had been her father.

Megan slid closer to Carl's body. The solidity of his frame and the heat rising from his skin comforted her. *There may be a reason why he can't love,* she thought, *a reason that has to do with the hyacinth woman or his illness.* But she knew Carl would not open up to her; he would not share his weakness with a young woman. She would have to return to Carl's mother for more information. He had kept even her existence a secret. Did he think she would pity the circumstances under which he lived? He mentioned that he would be alone for the winter. Alone to watch his mother die, alone perhaps to have his own health fail, or worse, to die himself. Alone. No one would miss him.

Careful not to awaken him, Megan reached over and clasped his hand. Even in sleep, his grasp tightened and he spoke somnolent words that didn't form clear sentences. It didn't matter, because she would stay with him, allowing him to feel the love she felt for him.

Chapter 26
Spl-a-t

Such a helpful young woman, Beverly thought as she sat on the garden swing. Ah! And Megan was a young woman, not a child. A woman who cared a great deal for a man, a son, someone's son, though certainly not Beverly's.

A sly chuckle came from in Beverly's throat.

"Son, indeed. I have more pride than to bed my own flesh and blood," she chattered. "I, too, have opened to this man, Megan, presenting to him my softest, sweetest charms. Even now, he desires me. He couldn't wait the other day to be captured between my fetid thighs." A guttural snort intruded on the soliloquy. "And what will you do, Megan, when he comes back to me again? Give him back to me or try to hold him? But you're too delicate, too fresh and clean for him. He prefers his women rotting and cold, without the ability to respond, because he must have it all. He doesn't share even his orgasm. No, he spills and splits." Beverly's hoarse laugh shook her black-draped body. "Yet there may be things we can do for each other. I can take the man and give you life. And that's exactly what will happen."

Beverly looked around the garden at hyacinths and roses stretching their slender necks up into the night, pushing through the stifling air of summer, blossoming into rainbow colors while their leaves yellowed and browned along the stem.

The bush behind the swing rustled; however, the rat therein remained unseen. The quiet onslaught of the undertaker, who cleans by feeding on decaying waste, had begun.

Beverly had opened her robe earlier that night when she first ventured into the garden to inspect the work Megan had done. The tools rested beside Beverly on the seat. They were coated with soil. Beverly spread the robe wide, offering her body to the moon, which, with the passing of a cloud, seemed to shut its eyes on what it saw.

Megan would come back again to save Carl, although Beverly knew that Megan would really be rescuing herself. She was not a very intelligent woman. Beverly caught these words passing through her thoughts. *Who are you to talk, "mother"? Your "son" leaves you here to rot slowly, and you accuse Megan of stupidity. I'll take him with me to hell. I'll see to it that every flame licks his body and blackens the silver of his hair. He'll be tarnished and wrinkled, with no one to visit him and desire the pungent smell of his charred skin. I've found the way, Carl. Megan is my way. And you've handed her to me. Therefore, you must want the end, no?*

Confused, Beverly touched her barren pate, an ethereal contact with her right hand, the palm not quite resting against her skull. The sleeve of the robe fell back onto the bone where the skin of her elbow used to be. A joint protruded instead. Stillness settled upon the figure. Washed again in the moon's incandescence, her skin, bloated and open, shimmered with a liquid glow.

Her mind empty, her soul poised, the body fragile in its decay, no sound of bird, beast, or brush shaking the timber of her world. All blissful in the emptiness.

A jolt charged through her brain. Was she already dead? Had she lost Carl forever? Another snap of electric charge crashed the remaining synapses. If she were dead, why was she still here? Why hadn't that cliché of a light led her forth into pleasure or, at the very least, oblivion? A current of pain wavered in and out of her memory. No, she wasn't finished; that was real, the vague trembling of neurons.

Beverly looked down at her right thigh and saw a small, dark brown rat chewing and swallowing. Nosing its head into her thigh, its fangs ripped into the shredding skin.

Ah! You brought me back to life, she pronounced silently.

And her hand descended, casting hardly a shadow on nature's creature enveloped in his professional task, doing his best for ecology. Not until it was too late did he realize he had clocked in too soon, for the hand gathered him up, allowing his fur to squeeze between digits. The rat snarled and flashed its fangs; no retreat here, only brutal combat with his prey.

Beverly's hand closed tighter around nature's living sweeper, hearing the joints go in and out of the sockets, the quiescent popping of tiny bones and cartilage. From where did she get the madness of her strength? Fascinated, Beverly compressed the wriggling animal tighter.

"Spl-a-t," she pronounced as the goo from her right hand dripped down on the gaping hole of her thigh.

Chapter 27
Purloined Sketch Pads

Heated by the sun, the two naked bodies slept on the bed, but neither stirred. The female kept one hand resting on the hirsute chest of the male, as if feeling, one would suppose, for a heartbeat. The male lay with arms stretched above his head, his hands matted into his silvery-golden hair. Their top cover lay in a wrinkled ball at the foot of the bed, allowing the warm breath of the summer morning to float across their bodies through the glassless window.

Carl raised his arms and pressed his palms against the red mahogany of the headboard. His eyes opened, then shut immediately against the daylight glare. Megan, awakened by his movement, lay watching him, shaded by the bulk of his body. Slowly her fingers drew small circles around the areola of his nipple.

Carl rolled over atop Megan and took her quickly, inconsiderately. Megan didn't respond or protest; instead, she accepted his weight, confused and alarmed at her lack of willpower.

"Great way to begin the morning," he said once the act was completed.

Megan felt their sticky bodies peel apart, smelled his maleness coming from inside her, a sour odor that overwhelmed the perfume of the hyacinths, and she wondered at his remote expression so soon after their intimacy.

Kneeling before her on the mattress, Carl stretched his arms wide, his pectorals rising as his stomach and abdomen flattened into perfection.

"Come lie next to me for a while, Carl."

"What?" He placed his fists on his waist. "You still tired or horny? Which is it?"

"I want to talk to you."

Carl's face turned taciturn. Obviously, he'd had many talks with women in bed and didn't want to have another, at least not that morning.

"I've got to finish some work today. Can't we talk at the breakfast table?"

"No!"

There was silence before Carl moved backward on the mattress, grabbing Megan's ankles as his feet touched the floor. With a strong yank, he pulled Megan's bottom to the edge of the bed. Laughing, he scooped her up and carried her into the bathroom.

"A cold shower is what you need, my little nymphomaniac."

Megan's slim body slid down Carl's taut muscles until her feet touched the cool white tiles. Reaching past her, Carl turned on the faucets, then lifted her pliant body into the tub, settling her directly under the spray of the showerhead.

The water was tepid. Megan felt Carl step in behind her.

"A little more hot, or would you prefer cold?" he asked, blowing his words into her ear.

"I wanted to talk, Carl."

"Right. Go ahead. I can do two things at once." Immediately he started to lather the soap in his hands. Then, with one hand, he held the soap while the other slid beneath the arch of her breast.

"Well, I . . . I . . ."

After lathering up again, Carl plopped the soap back into its dish, then started sudsing every curve of her figure.

Suddenly the heat of her body exploded into four simple words. "I have no protection."

"What?"

"I discontinued my birth-control pills after I broke up with my boyfriend."

"You think you might be pregnant?"

Megan had expected him to be annoyed. Instead, he leaned farther into her, stroking her body more lasciviously than before. Could he actually want her to be pregnant? she wondered. Was this the desperate need of man to continue his life through his progeny? Against the cheeks of her behind, Megan could feel his powerful excitement pressing into her. Willingly, Megan bent forward, bracing her hands against the yellowing tiles. Mildew crawled through the ancient grout. Water splashed against her neck, then slid down her collarbone and over her breast, heightening her sensitivity.

The pairing was long and lustful, finally satisfying Megan's physical desires but not her emotional ones. She knew so little about this man.

Megan lingered in the shower, listening to Carl's towel flap across his skin.

"I'll start breakfast," he said. And he was gone.

Later, after drying off and dressing, Megan followed the invisible, but sharp, pungent trail of coffee into the kitchen. Carl was scrambling some eggs; bacon was already draining into a paper towel, and toast was piled up on a plate on the center of the table. Megan took a slice, noticing that the underside had already been buttered.

"Shall I pour some juice?"

With a smile lifting up the corners of his mouth, Carl nodded. His eyes were bright, the blue majestically emboldened by the white surrounding it.

"Are you working at home today?"

"No, I'm going into town, still have to get that windowpane."

Megan wiggled her nose. Should she bother to ask?

"May I join you? I'm an excellent rower. Could save up some of your energy that way."

"For what?" he asked lustily.

Megan flushed; she hadn't meant it the way he had taken it.

"I'd like to see the town, and besides, wouldn't it be better to have company? The other day while you were working on the house down the river, I could have helped." She was testing him. Would he admit that he hadn't been alone?

"When I start working on the house, I don't notice anything around me. Besides, you're a guest. I'm not going to put you to work. That would make me an ungracious host, would it not?"

"Gracious hosts don't abandon their guests for long periods of time, Carl. Also, if I'm staying, I'd like to get some condoms."

"Why?"

"So I don't get pregnant."

"You're not going to get pregnant by me, Megan. I'm sterile. You also don't have to worry about catching anything. I had a physical examination shortly before you arrived."

"You got a clean bill of health from the doctor?"

"Although I have no certificate to prove it, I can assure you that I have nothing that you can catch from direct contact with me."

So whatever he had wasn't contagious, but he

wasn't saying that his health was perfect. Megan pondered this, wondering whether he could be ill with cancer, a bad heart. It could be any number of ailments.

"Eggs?"

Megan looked down at the plate Carl held out to her.

"They're a little runny."

"I don't like my eggs overdone. If you want, I can throw yours back in for a few more minutes."

She took the plate and walked to the table, ignoring his question.

"I guess not," she heard him mutter.

"Oh, they're fine. My roommate at school used to cook eggs until they started turning brown. Thought she was cooking away all the salmonella."

"Ugh!"

Megan bent her left leg across the chair and sagged down upon it while centering her plate on the watermelon-colored mat.

"It would be much faster if I went alone, Megan. I still need to do some more work for my project, and I don't want to waste time hanging around that old town."

Maybe he has a doctor's appointment, Megan guessed. Of course, he wouldn't want her to tag along, waiting in some dreary, brown office while he was being examined.

"Okay, I'll catch up on my reading while you're gone, but first tell me what you had planned for dinner."

"Dinner? Megan, we haven't even finished breakfast, and you're thinking about dinner?"

"So I can have it ready when you come back."

He laughed. "I won't be gone that long."

"You were gone quite a while the other day, and if you have to wait . . . I mean, wait to have the glass cut."

"David is hardly ever busy. He sits and reads most of the day; I don't know how he even pays' his rent."

"What if there's an emergency, and he's away replacing a houseful of broken windowpanes?"

"Megan, this is the middle of the summer. People appreciate the flow of a cool breeze."

"What if they have air-conditioning?"

"Hardly anyone around here could afford that luxury. But if hordes of neighbors should delay me on the street to ask how I am, unlikely as it might be, then you can throw together whatever you find that's still edible in the refrigerator."

"Do you have friends locally?" Megan asked after swallowing a particularly runny piece of egg.

"I keep to myself."

"Why?"

"Because I'm very private and don't like to have to answer too many questions."

Heeding the message, Megan changed the direction of the conversation.

"Is book two of your journal in the office?"

"Almost finished with the first?"

"Close."

"It's on the second shelf from the top in the bookcase near the window."

"Thanks."

Later, Megan waved good-bye as Carl rowed downstream toward the town. Carl hadn't noticed that the first journal still sat on the small boulder near the water. Megan walked over and picked the book up, shoving it between her elbow and rib cage so that she could jam her hands into the side pockets of her jeans. She walked up the path, taking a detour where the hyacinth smell was strongest. She found the mound. It appeared drier and dustier. After clearing a spot for herself in the grass, Megan sat and read.

By noon, she was famished. Carl hadn't returned as yet. She went down by the river to peer into the horizon, but saw no rowboat making its way back home. Assuming that he would miss lunch, Megan went back up to the house to prepare her own meal.

As she climbed the steps, she noticed a small nest on the tree limb overhanging the house. Two little heads bobbed up and down, chirping out their request for food. Megan placed a hand over her own stomach.

"I know how you feel," she said as her stomach's growling joined the chorus of chirps.

An adult bird descended on the nestlings, delivering their predigested lunch.

Megan, who had dabbled a bit in art while in school, was suddenly filled with the need to sketch this tender scene. But without paper or pencil . . . *Wait*, she thought, she had noticed that one or two of the sketch pads in the box in the bedroom were half empty.

Megan pulled open the screen door and rushed to the closet. She reasoned that Carl would never notice the missing sketch pads. It was probably too painful for him to go through the material contained in them.

After retrieving the two pads with the greatest number of empty pages, Megan folded up the box. She could sketch not only the nest, but also the garden. Maybe even get Carl's mother to pose for her. She was curious to see what that woman looked like under all that garb she wore.

Chapter 28
Ted

Carl slowly rowed downstream, enjoying the solitude. Megan was quite gullible. He had lied about being sterile. True, he had not fathered any children that he knew of, but he also had no reason to believe he was sterile. She might be the experimental subject he had longed to attract. If she was pregnant, how long would the process last? Would it be slower because two lives were giving themselves up to save him? But if she left, how would he know whether she was pregnant or not? Would she attempt to re-contact him to share the decision about what to do with the child? That was the last thing he wanted; after all, that might get others involved. Her father was dead, and she didn't get along with her mother, but she did have friends.

Perhaps female friends who could take her

place. What was he thinking? It was becoming much too complicated. The simplest solution was to try to talk her into staying. Offer her the yellow house, rent-free. Ah, yes!

Carl brought himself back to reality. She's not going to want to leave your bed, especially if she's pregnant. Carl thought of her rotting body next to him. No, he couldn't bear to have death so near on a constant basis. These thoughts triggered off his memories of Beverly. He was very near her house now. Should he stop and pay another visit? Making love was probably out of the question after his hedonistic morning, but he could look in on her and measure how much longer she had. He had felt no weakening inside his own body, no indication that her time was near the end; yet he was drawn to the rental house. Drawn by the dream of Beverly whole. However, only fragments of the woman were left. Bits and pieces held together by a will that refused to pass on, maybe even by a confused soul that didn't expect the early demise.

He had promised to pray for Beverly when it was time to dispose of her remains. Out of respect for her, he would mouth the useless words, but Carl was not religious. He believed the end was final. The white lights that were part of near-death experiences were nothing, just flashes sparking inside the brain before the blackness fell. Beverly had expressed agnostic views. Carl laughed, thinking that now she probably was a believer in a Supreme Being.

That's the way it was so many times when people were close to death. When he had been told that he was terminal, friends tried to preach to him, to pull him into a religious fold, whatever it might be, so that he could die a more peaceful death, patiently sitting in a pew at church or acknowledging the last rites of some drab zealot.

He looked toward the trees and saw the vague outline of the yellow house, standing quietly, looking empty and abandoned.

Did Beverly believe she had been deserted, discarded by the man she loved? It was tempting to stop. He had not reacted this way with the other women. It had been easy to leave them behind. Beverly was different. Carl shook his head. He loved her. After all the womanizing years he had spent prior to his disease and after, he finally had fallen in love, or at least cared for someone.

The rowboat was motionless in the water. Carl, holding the oars, had dropped his fists between his thighs, mesmerized by the bright yellow of the house under the rays of the sun. His love was there, dying his death. Carl shook out the tension from his shoulders, lowered the oars, and settled them back into the water. He had to go into town and be back early enough to work in the study. He didn't want Beverly to have sacrificed in vain.

As the rowboat moved through the water, Carl tried to envision Megan. Had he missed any of her essential markings or scars? The photographs, once developed, would help with her overall general appearance, but often a blemish or slight defect might go unnoticed by the lens.

Ravens squawked above a cluster of trees, zeroing in on the carcass waiting to be picked. *Above ground or below ground, the scavengers eventually get you,* Carl thought. He spat out his distaste for the birds into the river.

Perspiration soaked the back of his cotton shirt, reaching up to mingle with the wetness already spreading out in his armpits. His white linen trousers were wrinkled. Like a magnet, the linen had attracted the bit of dirt and oil coating the inside of the boat. His muscles flexed easily under the thin layer of clothing. Dark brown sandals sat on the board across from Carl waiting to be fitted onto his bare feet.

Up ahead, someone called his name. It was the widower Morgan's ten-year-old son, Ted. Carl was always generous with the boy, taking him into town to buy a toy or piece of clothing that the boy needed. It was the least Carl could do after the boy's mother had wasted away mysteriously. That was the last and only time Carl had allowed his secret to be displayed in public. If that happened too many times to women Carl dated, either on the sly or in public, he was sure he would find the sheriff hounding him.

"How are you doing today?" Carl asked as he moved in to shore.

"Okay." The boy sounded sullen. Often his father would disappear for a day or two on a drunken binge. Ted's old man had lost his job six months after his wife's death. The town tolerated his reprehensible behavior because of the boy and the hideousness of the mother's death.

"You have breakfast this morning?"

"Wasn't hungry."

Just as Carl had thought; the kid's useless father was gone again.

"I have to pick up some things, but you know, I got awfully hungry rowing today."

"Yeah?"

"Would you like to join me at the diner for some lunch?"

Ted nodded enthusiastically.

"Then let's go."

Carl secured the rowboat, then took Ted's hand.

The child's hand was small, with slivers of flesh for fingers. After his mother died, Ted had steadily lost weight until he had stabilized into a scrawny child. Carl had briefly thought of sketching Ted when he was plump and while the mother was decomposing, but Carl had liked the boy. About the only child he had liked. Mainly because the boy was quiet and shy enough to keep what he saw to himself.

The child must have been aware of the afternoon visits to his mother, Carl knew, yet he was sure that Ted had never spoken of them before or after her death, either to his father or anyone else. The kid didn't look like either of his parents, and knowing the mother the way he had, Carl believed it was quite possible that his father was not the man she had married. Carl viewed Ted as an orphan to be comforted.

"Why don't we kill two birds with one stone? I have to pick up some groceries, so after we eat why don't we both do our shopping for the week."

"Dad doesn't like—"

"Tell him family dropped them off."

"But they don't like Dad."

"They still like you, don't they?" *When they bother to see you,* he said to himself.

"Aunt Bea dropped by last week. Didn't stay long, though; Dad was in a bad mood."

Dad was drunk, Carl silently corrected, *as he usually is.*

Ted continued his story about Aunt Bea's visit while they walked down the street toward the one and only diner in town.

By late afternoon, Carl was waving good-bye to Ted as his rowboat made its way upstream, with the pane of glass precariously tied across one end of the small vessel. Underneath the glass Carl had laid out the groceries he had bought for himself and Megan. Ted had been curious about the amount of produce Carl was buying. Sharp for a kid, thought Carl, but it hadn't been difficult to divert the boy's attention by stopping at the candy shelves. Ted now had enough food to last the rest of the week. By then, maybe his family would visit again or perhaps Carl would stop back in town. Anyway, Carl was confident that the boy wouldn't have to share much of the food with his old man, since Carl had also placed a couple of bottles of scotch in the kitchen cupboard. That would be sufficient for the father's dinners. Carl didn't want the widower sober and asking questions.

The rowboat floated deep in the water. Carl rowed slowly so that he wouldn't cause any splash. Smoothly the oars worked the river.

He hadn't planned on returning home so late, but he could never ignore Ted. Neither could he turn away from the sight of the yellow house that was almost camouflaged by the trees. He gaped, knowing he would not see Beverly, but was unable to accept that as a fact.

He realized with a start that the boat was moving in the direction toward which he was looking. Carl quickly corrected the swerve of the boat and moved on toward home and Megan.

Chapter 29
Revenge

Beverly had spent the day waiting. She gave up hope when the sun's rays no longer made her skin hiss when she drew close to the window. Megan wasn't coming today. Would she ever come again? Had she disobediently told Carl about seeing his so-called mother? Beverly couldn't fathom what a scatterbrain like Megan would do.

Beverly closed the slats on the living-room window. There wasn't anything to see now that the sun was retiring for the night. Her dark robe clung to her decaying flesh as she walked back to her bedroom, where she pulled open the curtains on the French doors. She was tempted to unlock those doors and throw them wide for the rats to tumble through, allowing them to feast on her. Yet she couldn't bring herself to do that, not because of cowardice, but for the sake of revenge, which she knew existed somewhere. She had thought to use Megan for that purpose, but if the young woman didn't return, she would have to find another way.

Was it a sob that heaved her breast? Beverly wondered. No, she wouldn't say "if" Megan would return. Megan would come back because of curiosity, and mainly love. Love for a man who would destroy her.

She looked out through the glass of the French doors and saw several rats sniffing nearby. They dodged a mazelike trail through the grass, then stopped like stone statues, with only whiskers vaguely twitching.

"I'm here, guys, but you'll have to wait, because I've got another rat to deal with before you fellows can have me."

Beverly took hold of the doorknob and lowered herself gently down to her knees and prayed. Not for mercy or forgiveness, but for retribution.

Chapter 30
A Request

After helping Carl install the new windowpane, Megan spent the evening preparing a late-night candlelit dinner, which paid off by keeping Carl from his work. Instead he was warm, almost tender, in the way he spoke to her and catered to her own sexual needs.

That night she slept blissfully next to Carl with the sketch pads she had selected squirreled away under the mattress. Her plan was to encourage Carl's work and sneak off with the rowboat by ten o'clock.

She didn't have to make any attempt to carry out her plan, however, since Carl rose before her, leaving a note on the kitchen table informing her that he was not to be disturbed while he was working.

"Please, Carl, could you be any less eager to

wish me a good morning?" She sighed as she crumpled the note and threw it into the trash. "A quick breakfast, then off I go," she continued with forced brightness.

Megan poured some cereal flakes into a bowl and doused it heavily with skimmed milk. Using a paring knife, Megan toppled chunks of banana into the bowl. By the time she had finished, the coffeepot had perked. Hardly tasting the food, Megan finished her breakfast, then left the plates in the sink and made for the study.

Leaning an ear against the door, Megan could hear nothing. She wanted to knock and call out "Have a good day," but his note had been so curt that she didn't dare.

Instead, Megan returned to the bedroom and slipped the sketch pads from their hiding place. Both were still perfectly flat, since they had been squeezed between the box spring and a heavy mattress.

"Now to sneak out without being seen," she whispered.

In the kitchen she put some fruit, cheese, and bread into a brown paper bag along with a diet soda. She found several freshly sharpened pencils in a drawer. She was hesitant about leaving the breakfast dishes in the sink, but figured it wouldn't matter since they were piled on top of Carl's, so she assumed he wasn't fastidious about these things. Megan tiptoed out of the kitchen, past the study, and toward the front door. Once outside, she started to charge down the path, feeling like a sneak thief.

She didn't feel comfortable until she climbed the path leading to the yellow house. The slats on the jalousie definitely moved; that was no trick of the sun. The old woman must have been waiting for her to come. Megan waved, even though she wasn't sure if the woman still stood in the front room or had already gone around back to the garden.

As she got closer, she noticed a medium-size bag of fertilizer on the top step. When she reached to pick it up, she saw that it was covered with dew from the night before. *Oh, no! She probably waited all day yesterday for me, the poor dear,* Megan thought guiltily.

Thinking she could make up for the delayed visit by offering to sketch the elderly woman, Megan tightened her hold on the pads, which she held between her body and left arm. One of the pads started to slip as she awkwardly rounded the house, fertilizer firmly gripped in both hands.

"Hi," she called out as the pads fell to the earth just outside the garden gate. Megan shifted the bag into her left arm so that she could unlatch the gate. She pushed it open with her healing knee, remembering the wound only after a twinge of pain.

"I'm back."

At first Megan could not see the elderly woman. The French doors were open, but no one seemed to be there. She caught a glimpse of a black leather hand grasping the side of one of the doors.

"It's me. Megan. The one you left the fertilizer out for," she called, wondering whether the bag had indeed been left out for her. What if the old woman was senile and couldn't remember people she talked to from day to day?

"Megan, I was afraid you weren't coming back." There was true fear tightening that hoarse voice. "You didn't tell Carl about me, did you?"

"Of course not. He's busy working in the study on some important project of his today, so I crept away to see you. Your son really gets involved with his work. It's impossible to distract him. I guess you're proud of what he does.

"I haven't had a chance to see any of his photographs as yet." Megan blushed a bit, thinking about what those photographs would contain. "But I'm looking forward to seeing some soon." This wasn't a lie. Megan had never seen herself photographed in the buff before and wondered how she would compare to some of those centerfolds she had seen.

"He took pictures of you?" The old woman seemed to be wheezing badly.

Megan hesitated. Could his mother guess at what had happened? Then again, her son was no child, and Megan had already admitted that she was staying at his small house.

"Yes. Maybe he'll develop them today while I'm gone."

"I'm sure he will," the woman said wisely. "He likes duplicating the women around him."

212

What a strange way of putting it, thought Megan, but she was old, and all this photography business may have seemed unusual to her.

"Ma'am?"

"Call me Beverly, please."

"Beverly, would you like me to work on anything in particular today?"

Beverly's hand motioned toward the cluster of hyacinths.

Megan had many questions to ask Beverly, but she decided to work in the garden first while the morning was still cool. Beverly withdrew into her home, leaving Megan to work at her own pace.

At one o'clock Megan stopped to eat her lunch out of the brown paper bag. After lunch, since it was the hottest part of the day, Megan walked across the garden to collect her sketch pads. She cleared off the garden swing and sat with her back to the sun, sketching the yellow house and the shrubbery that guarded the French doors.

When Megan was just about finished and ready to turn the page to move on to a new subject, she heard what sounded like gas hissing from a pipe.

"What are you doing?" rasped Beverly from the center of the doorway.

"I was sketching. I used to do it a lot when I was younger. It always relaxed me. I could sketch you if you'd like. Perhaps you'd like Carl to have a likeness of you. But then, since he is a photographer, I guess he's taken many snapshots of you."

"He has only one likeness of me, but he said he did it from memory."

"Did what from memory? Did he try his hand at sketching, too?"

"You mean like you?"

"Carl told me about the woman he lived with and about how she used to have models come to the house so that she could sketch them. Actually, this is one of her pads."

Beverly reached out with a gloved hand, moving forward until the sun hit the drabness of her robe. Stung by the burning rays, her body wilted, shoulders visibly lowered; her hand fell to the front fold of the material, her shawled face dropped lower onto her chest, and her knees started to buckle.

"Here, let me help you."

Megan jumped up from the swing, dropping the pad onto the ground, and moved forward quickly to catch the old woman. As Megan's arms encircled the dark form, Beverly exhaled the cry that had almost caused her to collapse, and with it a stench filled the air, forcing Megan to free her. Horror-stricken, Megan watched as Beverly raised her hand to her face. Were those maggots she saw squirming down the gloved hand? Megan shook her head and closed her eyes. It couldn't be.

When she opened her eyes again, no one was standing in front of her and the sweet smell of hyacinths had again settled around her.

"The pad," called Beverly from the bedroom. "Bring me the pad, Megan, now. I want it now."

Seeing the woman so hysterical, Megan quickly ran to retrieve the sketches. At arm's length she handed the pad to Beverly and watched as the woman flipped violently through the pages, tearing the spiraled edges as she did. The old woman appeared to be panting for air.

O my God, please don't let her have a heart attack now, Megan prayed. *I wouldn't know what to do, and it would certainly have been all my fault.*

"I didn't mean to upset you, honest," Megan pleaded, hoping she could soothe the woman's temper. *I should have known that Beverly wouldn't have liked that hyacinth woman, and here I am bringing the sketches right to her door,* she thought. *What a pea-brain you are, Megan.*

Soon Beverly reached Megan's sketch.

"You draw well, Megan. Perfect, absolutely perfect."

"It's far from perfect. Are you all right now?"

"Fine! Much better! You've given me joy again."

Scratching her curly ringlets, Megan backed away from the doorway.

"I guess I'll finish up here and head back. You can keep the pad if you want."

"Oh, no! I want you to use the pad, Megan. I want you to draw Carl."

"Okay, but I'm not sure it would be appropriate for me to ask him to sit for something like that, given how he felt about that woman," she said, nodding toward the pad.

"No, you mustn't tell him. Memorize him. Memorize every part of him."

"Gee, I could probably sketch out his face now if you'd like."

"No! Not just the face. I want a naked drawing of him."

Megan's eyes widened. "Naked?"

"Yes. He has a mole right about here," Beverly said, indicating a very private part of the anatomy.

I guess she is his mother, Megan thought. *Mothers do change diapers.*

"It must be a perfect replica. Search his body with your hands and eyes. Learn every detail of his form and skin."

Megan's cheeks were afire. What could she say? She was so flustered that she couldn't deny she had been intimate with this woman's son.

"Please. I need it, Megan."

Megan recalled that the woman had said that Carl was ill. Maybe she wanted this drawing to remind her of him after he died. But naked! Well, didn't all mothers have bearskin-rug-type photographs of their babies? *Even at fifty, he's still her baby,* Megan declared silently.

She nodded. As she did, she moved closer to Beverly to take back the pad that was held out to her.

"It might take a few days."

"I want it perfect. If it means waiting a few days, that's all right."

As she took back the pad, Megan tried to peek under the heavy shawl, but all she could make out was some blackened skin covering a sharp chin.

Chapter 31
Don't Forget the Shovel

In a puddle of maggots Beverly watched Megan close the garden gate behind her. Squirming larvae worked their way down Beverly's nasal passages and up through her throat, freeing themselves from the rotting flesh within. Beverly spat the fatted chunks of squiggly debris onto the ground in front of her.

She would have to be more careful, carry a handkerchief with her, so that Megan would not see what was spewing up from within her. Beverly had finally found her means of vengeance, but she didn't want to scare the messenger away before the time had come to act.

"Those rats have heavy competition," she

said, staring down at the whirling life surrounding her booted feet.

Somehow, Beverly had managed to distance herself from the decay and rot. She couldn't explain the aloofness she experienced as she watched what was happening to her body. Had she been driven mad? No, she confessed, it wasn't lunacy driving her; it was the desire to stop Carl.

"You may never know who the person was who destroyed you, Carl, but that's not what matters. Survival will come out of this for one of us three." She gagged on the rubbish crawling up her throat. "You'll die a worse death than what could have been back in the Amazon."

Beverly swayed back and forth in the stillness of the bedroom as she surveyed the garden. The tools were beneath the swing where Megan had placed them.

"A shovel!"

She turned away from the afternoon sunlight and headed back into the depths of the house to search for a shovel. Scattered about an unfurnished room was a multitude of apparatus, some of which no longer had any reason to be there. Then there were the tools that hadn't been touched since Carl had fixed up the house for rental. But no shovel.

"It's just like you, Carl, to hide all the equipment necessary for your spells. But now I have an ally who'll help me. I'm sure you have shovels of various sizes stuck away in your own house. Megan shouldn't find it difficult to whisk one away from you."

Beverly went to the living room, opened the slats on the window, and watched the calm afternoon change into a breezy summer evening. When twilight began flickering through the room, Beverly heard some shuffling sounds coming from the bedroom. Sensing her nightly visitors were back, Beverly gently shut the jalousie and retreated slowly to the bedroom, where she saw several rats nuzzling the bed linen, which was balled up on the floor.

"I'm not there, you fools," she rasped as she lurched into the room, scattering the rats.

One rat, which had climbed to the top of the armoire, leaped down upon her, fixing its teeth on the side of her neck under the long shawl. The other rats, gaining confidence from their confederate, advanced on her, mouths atwitter in their warring cries.

Chapter 32
Moonlight Swim

Megan sat on the lid of the toilet, sketching feverishly. *No, that's not right,* she grumbled as she corrected the shape of Carl's chin, then erased the tuft of hair sticking out from behind the base of his skull. Carl had just trimmed his own hair; that silly little bit of silver-blond was gone now. Something about the nose didn't look quite right to her, either. Perhaps she had made it too large or—wait, it wasn't straight enough.

Eraser crumbs were sprinkled across her naked feet and overflowed onto the floor's tiles. Her toes wiggled excitedly as she attempted to perfect the drawing.

"Damn," she cursed.

"Megan, are you all right?"

Shortly after dinner, Carl had excused himself from the table and had said that he would be working in the study for a while. For some reason that Megan couldn't fathom, he had taken the developed photographs with him. Earlier he had surprised her with both negatives and photographs. After viewing them, Megan tried to think of a way to steal the negatives. She certainly wouldn't want them published or lost. Burned was the best answer. However, Carl had put them away in the study in one of the locked drawers. Oh well, Megan had thought, at least this gave her a chance to begin her own project for his mother. Megan had loaded the sink with dishes and retreated to her own private office.

"Megan, are you ill?"

She hurriedly flipped the pad shut, placed it on the edge of the bathtub, and began unwinding a chunky roll of toilet paper.

"Be right out," she called as she started to dampen the paper.

Squatting down, Megan cleaned off first her feet, then the tiles. She wanted no casual evidence left behind. When she was finished, she flushed the paper down the toilet, hid the pad behind the pedestal sink, then threw open the door, walking directly into Carl.

"Sorry."

"Are you all right? You've been in there for quite a while."

"Not very long, really."

"I stopped working a half hour ago, and

you've been sequestered in there ever since."

"I'm fine." Megan shrugged as if the world were hunky-dory.

Carl started to move around her to enter the bathroom. Megan reached her hand across the doorway, gripping the frame.

"Where are you going?"

"Mind if I use my own bathroom?"

"Why don't you use the one off the hall?" she said, envisioning the edges of the pad protruding on either side of the pedestal.

"What's the difference?"

"I'm taking a bath."

"A dry one," he said, looking her up and down.

"Well, I was about to take a bath."

"Is that what you were pondering so long in the bathroom?"

"Sort of."

"Take your bath," he said, holding his hands palms-outward in front of him.

Once Carl was out of the room, Megan raced back into the bathroom to retrieve the sketch pad. She had just barely slipped it under the mattress when she heard Carl's returning footsteps.

"I thought you were taking a bath."

"Changed my mind."

Carl shook his head.

"Shall we walk down to the river?"

"What are you going to do, bathe in the river instead?"

Megan giggled and teasingly brushed her hand against his cheek.

"Maybe we can go for a moonlight swim," she said seductively. She immediately caught herself. A midnight swim wouldn't allow her to see any of the specifics of his body, but it was too late to retract the offer, because he accepted immediately.

Megan wondered if she was right to be so fanatical. Was it really necessary to have a perfect likeness to give to Beverly? Would Beverly know the difference? Doubtful, she thought, but she had promised, and Megan would feel guilty of cheating if the drawing was not exact. Okay, maybe she could delay the lovemaking until they got back to the bedroom, so they could perform under the glare of a one-hundred-watt lightbulb. *How unromantic*, she objected to herself.

"Do you live alone, Megan?"

They were on the path that led to the river. She didn't even remember walking out of the house, because she had been so caught up in her own thoughts.

"Excuse me?"

"Do you live alone?"

"No. Hester and I are roommates. Actually, we've been best friends since the third grade."

"I guess you'd like to live alone for a while."

"No. I'd have no one to share the chores with and I'd have to clean the house, do the laundry, and go food shopping every week. With Hester,

I do those only every other week, and sometimes I barter myself an extra free week here and there. I probably did two-thirds of her research for school while we were in college. Since I was going to the library anyway, I'd offer to do some research for her while I was there if she did my chores for that week."

"Didn't know you were so lazy."

Megan scowled. "I'm only lazy when it comes to housework. The problem is, I think like a man." She watched Carl's eyebrows rise. "I bet the dinner dishes are still in the sink."

"You put them there."

"Ah, and you had, by your own admission, at least a half hour in which to do them."

Carl laughed. "I'm guilty. There have been times that dishes have sat in the sink until I've run out of clean dinnerware."

Megan stuck her tongue out at him.

"How inviting," he whispered, rounding her waist with his left arm.

Flustered, Megan stumbled over her feet, but Carl lifted her up into his arms before she could fall. He carried her to the edge of the river.

"Should I drop you in, clothes and all?"

"No!" she screeched, enjoying the physical contact.

"Then why don't we peel each other's clothes off?" he said, letting her body slide down the length of him.

An hour later, Megan was no more cognizant of his every pore than she had been before. She had been so enmeshed in their love play that she hadn't even considered the promise she had made to Beverly. However, she was content and sated. Tomorrow evening she could act on her assignment if she wasn't lucky enough to get a replay tonight. She sighed.

"That's a heavy-duty sigh."

"I was thinking about how unfettered it feels to make love in the outdoors."

"I certainly haven't chained you to the bed yet," he said, the glint in his eye making Megan feel more secure about returning to the house for an encore.

"Maybe we should try it indoors now to compare." Megan began quickly scooping up their clothes.

"Take it easy, Megan. Throw me my jeans."

With an underhand throw, Megan tossed the jeans to Carl. They fell onto the ground, just short of his outreached hand.

"I was never good at sports. In gym class, I was always one of the last people to be chosen for a team. I was plenty popular socially, but all the kids knew I was clumsy once I got a ball in my hands."

Carl stood and slipped on his jeans, after which he reached into the bundle of clothes in Megan's arms to pull out his shirt.

"The rest is yours, I presume."

Megan started to dress also. When she was finished, Carl called to her. He was sitting on a large rock. As she approached, he moved over to make room for her.

"Do you like spending time in the country?"

"With you, definitely."

She watched his smile broaden. Very straight teeth, she noted. His tongue inched out to cover the front two teeth as if pausing to recoup some idea. He flashed her another smile.

"Why not stay through until next summer?"

"Carl—"

"There must be things you'd like to do. Are you even sure what kind of job you want to work at?"

"No, as a matter of fact, I have no idea what I'm going to do. I studied anthropology because I enjoyed it, but going off on expeditions to locate ancient cultures . . . I don't know. On this trip I haven't done too well. Could you imagine me in the jungles of some far-off place? Besides, I'd have to go to graduate school, which I can't afford right now."

"Then stay here and think awhile. Isolate yourself; learn who you are."

"Carl, I wouldn't be alone," she reminded him.

"If you stayed at the rental house, you would be."

Megan was about to deny that when she literally bit her tongue. Poor Beverly; did he expect his mother to pass on that soon? True, Beverly did appear to be wasting away from some disease. But on the other hand, she had told Megan that Carl was the one in poor health. Whether it was miscommunication or confusion, Megan knew something was wrong.

"I couldn't afford the rent. That's another one of the blessings about having a roommate, and I don't think Hester wants to be isolated."

"No, I don't want you bringing Hester here," he said a little too loudly. Calmly he continued, "You're young and you've had to take care of yourself for quite some time. Stay at the yellow house and sort out your possibilities. You could pay me minimum rent, or none at all if your money is tight."

"But doesn't the rent on that place help to pay the bills?"

"I have investments elsewhere that pay my bills, and I don't need much. I own the land and houses mortgage-free and need no luxuries, just the basics of food and utilities."

"Can I think about this?"

"Of course. That's the answer I was hoping for. I didn't expect you to accept immediately."

Later, in bed, when it was evident that Carl was recharged, Megan jumped off the sheet-covered mattress and flipped on the ceiling light.

"Why the spotlight?"

"Seeing you turns me on," she said, standing at the foot of the bed, her eyes soaking up the vision before her.

"Couldn't you do that with smaller wattage?" His voice was hesitant. Megan found it intriguing that she could make this mature, worldly man uncomfortable. She felt intrigued and powerful.

"The light stays on," she breathed.

For the first time, Megan's hands searched a man's body. Instead of being the submissive partner, she was the superior force in the coupling.

Chapter 33
Disappointment

Beverly's hand shook as she disrobed. Bits of rotted skin and cartilage clung to the dark fabric. The rats had managed to steal chunks of her flesh before she was able to kill every last one of the bastards. Blood left fingerlike trails on the walls behind her. At the floorboard rested the carcass of one of the rats, its head smashed and its guts ripped out by Beverly's own fingernails.

When attacked, Beverly had moved back into the hall, her hands violently flailing about her body, trying to detach the hungry mouths from her blood-soaked garment. Somehow she had managed to close the door separating the bedroom from the hallway, preventing any further attacks. She had spent the night in the hall mauling the remains. Few of her fingernails remained intact. One or two had broken off when she first had started to decay. Most of the others fell into the gaping holes she had clawed out in the rats' stomachs.

Dragging the dark, spattered robe along the floor, she opened the door and returned to the bedroom. Sunlight sprayed the floor golden. In this room there was no trace of the struggle. Beverly opened the mirrored door of the armoire. Silks, velvets, nylon, and cotton of deep hues hung across the wooden bar. Beverly dropped the robe to the floor. She pulled out a flimsy, see-through nylon garment. Its taffeta underdress had fallen onto the shoes that lined the floor of the armoire.

Inappropriate, she thought, but smiled. Something for Goodwill. Opening her hand, she let the sheer material drop to the floor. She needed much heavier cloth to shield her distress from Megan.

She saw that the shawl had not been damaged. A little blood stiffened the corner, but this she could hide. Her boots, although scuffed, were presentable. At least they still hid her decaying toes. Her piggies wiggled in childlike delight.

"One little piggy went to market. One little piggy stayed home. One little piggy . . ." Beverly faltered. The rhyme wasn't coming. "One I know had roast beef, and wasn't one forced to do without? But there should be five little piggies." Should she take off her boots and make sure all her piggies were there? Suppose one of the rats had huffed and puffed and snatched one, she pondered. But she didn't care much about her little piggies anymore; she was more interested in . . . She wondered for a few seconds. Megan. Yes, she thought; she didn't want to frighten Miss Megan away.

Her glance returned to the armoire. What to wear? When she reached out to finger the garments before her, she noticed the leather glove had a gash spreading down from the web of her thumb. Were her fingers nimble enough to sew up the seam? She opened and closed her hand. No, they were not. Ah, but she did have a dressy pair of cotton gloves that she had forgotten. Not since childhood and parochial school had she worn white gloves.

Beneath the open door of the armoire there was a huge, sticky drawer that groaned and squeaked when pulled open. Stooping, she jerked open one side of the drawer an inch, then the other side an inch, and on and on until the drawer's contents lay exposed.

She pushed her fingers under a frilly girl's petticoat and found the white gloves. Slowly Beverly lowered herself down onto her knees. Under a clear plastic cover the gloves shimmered in a ray of sunlight. Beverly unwrapped them. Her head tilted onto her left shoulder. They didn't look quite right. They fit before, but now they looked small. Way too small. Daintily, she placed a white glove atop the leather that covered her left hand. The palm of the white

glove covered only two-thirds of her palm. The
digits didn't even reach up halfway. Would they
stretch? she wondered. She laboriously skinned
the leather and top layer of flesh from her left
hand before trying to squeeze her fingers into
an opening that was meant for a child's hand.

Disappointed, Beverly sat herself down on
the floor. When had she worn them last? Was it
fourth grade for the Queen of the May celebra-
tion? *My God, it was!* Shocked, Beverly dropped
the gloves. This was many years later, wasn't it?
Drawing on all her memories, she sorted,
flipped through sheaves of acquaintances and
lovers. And then there was Carl. She growled
low like a hungry stray pretending strength.

Megan was coming. She had to keep remembering Megan. Megan was coming. Megan
would help her. Megan. She kept whispering
the name. Megan gave her a focus. Holding on
to the swinging door of the armoire, she managed to raise herself. "Megan," she whispered.
Megan. She must dress for Megan's visit.
Mustn't scare Miss Megan away. Megan. She
droned Megan's name out as a chant, she sang
Megan's name like a lullaby, she called to her
goddess, Megan. All the while, she searched the
armoire for something to wear. Finally, way in
the side and back of the armoire, she found a
ball of multicolor terry cloth. When she shook
the material out, it drooped from her hands to
the floor. It was an ugly old robe given her by a
maiden aunt years ago. The aunt had died, but

the vibrancy of her gift lived on within Beverly's grasp.

Beverly shut the mirrored door and pushed her arms through the sleeves of the bright robe. Tying the sash around her, she looked at her reflection. Orange balloons floated down across raspberry-colored shoulders. Stripes of primary colors across her bosom barricaded the descent of the balloons, which dangled hideously, not knowing where to go. The sash recovered the raspberry minus the balloons. "Thank God," she whispered. But the skirt shifted the stripes from horizontal to vertical.

Beverly thought about her aunt's sense of humor. Had she really believed that a grown woman would wear such a thing? she wondered. *You are wearing it*, she reminded herself, *and be glad you have it*.

Was her aunt coming? Is that why she wore this ugly thing? Someone was coming. Megan! *Megan is coming*, she happily remembered.

Quickly she adjusted the shawl so that it would shadow her face, preventing Megan from seeing the deteriorating effects of Carl's curse. The gloves. Could she remember to keep one hand in her pocket? Beverly looked down at the patches that acted as pockets and noticed the orange balloons covering them. Many of the balloons were embedded in the stitches bordering the pockets.

Beverly dragged the leather up over the rawness of her left hand, hoping the hole would be

234

smaller than she remembered. No, it had widened.

When Beverly heard the squeak of the garden gate, she was pulling undies and bras from a dresser drawer in her quest for gloves.

"Too late," she mumbled. "Megan's here."

Giddy, Beverly slammed shut the drawer and ran to the French doors, which had not been closed since the previous day.

"Megan," she gaily rasped out.

"Hi, Beverly."

Megan was dressed in a pair of denim cutoffs and a short-sleeved T-shirt with an advertisement for a sixties band lettered across two firm, full-size mounds. Beverly noticed how deeply the letters sagged in the middle. *Carl must be satisfied*, she thought. On her feet, Megan wore brown hiking boots over some thick, gray-speckled socks. Under her arm she carried a sketch pad.

Beverly quivered.

"Did you do the drawing? Did you? Is it complete? May I see it now?"

She knew the answer before Megan spoke. The girl's forehead furrowed; the light brows lowered over her brown eyes.

"It's not finished yet. I'm sorry, Beverly. I thought I could work on it some more today after I garden."

"Garden! The garden's fine. What's a weed or two? Draw, Megan. Draw my love for me."

The girl stared at her. Beverly reached down her hand self-consciously to help conceal the orange balloons on the pockets, but then, looking down, Beverly understood what was so appalling to Megan.

Beverly had forgotten the gash in the leather. Fluids and bits of raw, stale meat were protruding. Immediately the left hand dove inside the darkness of a balloon-covered pocket. She caught Megan's head bending, scooting low to see under the dark shawl shielding Beverly's face.

"Garden first, if it relaxes you, Megan. I have other things to do inside."

Casually Beverly glanced behind her and saw the hurricane of debris spewed across the floor and mattress.

"Cleaning, Megan. I'm cleaning up before the fall. I have a lot to do. Some things must go to charity. Perhaps you could see to it if I bundled a load of clothes?"

"Of course," Megan said softly with pity.

Dangerously close to the bright glare of the sun, Beverly faced Megan.

"Draw, Megan. You have to duplicate him for me." She watched the girl's head bob loosely. "It's for your own sake, too. We both need that drawing."

How could she impress the importance of this on the dippy girl? Frustrated, Beverly ran to her office, collected every pencil she could find, and rushed back to Megan with her hand extended, holding yellow sticks of offerings.

"Oh, I have plenty of pencils," Megan said as she settled her materials on the garden swing.

"Not only did I borrow, shall we say, two of the sketch pads, I also swiped quite a few pencils with good erasers. At least, they were good before I started to work."

"Erasers! Yes, I have erasers." Beverly dropped the pencils on the threshold of the door. Pencils rolled back into the house and away, out onto the grass.

A minute later she was back with two large, gray erasers.

Megan took the proffered gifts. Beverly caught sight of Megan's still chest as she approached. The girl was holding her breath to keep from smelling her. An incredible desire to reach out and grab Megan and hold her close was tempered by whatever reason Beverly had left. She needed Megan; mustn't frighten her away.

"Thank you, Beverly, I think I will try to draw for a while. Could I sketch you, perhaps as kind of a warm-up?"

Beverly gasped. "I've already been sketched, you stupid girl," Beverly shouted. Then her voice grew quiet as she said, "Probably you've already been sketched, too."

"By whom?"

"Moron, who would need to sketch you? The big, bad wolf, of course."

"I'm bright enough to know that wolves may eat people, but they certainly don't have the skill to draw."

"The warm, seductive ones do." Beverly giggled. "Do you know any charming wolves with sizable equipment?"

Beverly saw Megan's cheeks flush. The girl turned away and collected her materials from the swing.

"I'm sorry, Megan. Please don't go."

"I thought I could help you, but now I see you wanted to make a fool of me the whole time."

"No. No. I'm only warning you."

"To stay away from your son."

"No. I speak too freely sometimes, but I don't mean to hurt anyone." Beverly attempted a sniffle. Damn, she thought, not even a hankie in these stupid pockets. Beverly bowed her head and gently drew the sleeve of one arm across her hidden nose, careful not to lop anything off that might drive Megan away. "I'm so lonely here. Please, Megan, don't go away."

There was a low huff from the girl.

"Go and do whatever needs doing in the house. I'm going to garden before the sun gets too strong. After lunch I'll try sketching. Okay?"

Beverly gave a subtle, sad nod, turned, and walked with halting steps across the bedroom. From the doorjamb she called back to Megan. "Bring a shovel the next time you come. I can't find my own." Under her breath Beverly seethed that Carl had probably taken it the last time he was there. "I need to dig a hole for a new plant," she assured Megan. Once in the hallway and out of Megan's view, she began gleefully humming. Then she went to the kitchen to search for matches.

Chapter 34
Found

"Aren't you going to visit the yellow house?"

Carl raised his head from the book he was reading.

"What for?"

Megan placed her cereal spoon into the bowl, manipulating the soggy flakes.

"Didn't you have work to do on the place?"

"Not yet." He returned to the book.

"You really should visit."

Keeping his head bowed, Carl crinkled his brow so that he could glance up at Megan, who was sitting across from him at the kitchen table.

"Why?"

Megan scooped up a brimming spoonful of milk and flakes, but before slipping the spoon into her widening mouth, she spoke.

"To check on the place." Megan stretched out

her neck so that her mouth could clamp onto the spoon.

"Nothing's going to happen to the place, Megan." He raised his head. "Have you decided to stay?"

Dropping the spoon back into the bowl, Megan splashed her hand and white, long-sleeved sweatshirt. Quickly she dabbed the material with a napkin. She wriggled her rear in the chair, trying to get comfy in an extremely uncomfortable situation.

"Not exactly."

"You're leaning in that direction."

"I'm exploring the idea."

"Seriously?"

"Yes, but don't get your hopes up. Why don't you go there today and check out the place? Make sure someone can safely spend the winter there. For instance, when was the last time the furnace was used?"

"Last winter."

"Who was staying there?"

"A renter, of course."

"Do you have any family nearby?"

"No. I have no family, period. I was orphaned by both parents at the ripe old age of thirty-six; no siblings and no relatives with whom my parents were on speaking terms. A simple life history."

Megan watched Carl closely. He lied without flinching. His eyes were clear, blue, and innocent. Why wouldn't he admit that his mother was still at the yellow house? She recalled how sincere Beverly's plea was that she shouldn't tell Carl about their meeting. Megan wished she could yell it out and demand that he visit that poor woman before her mind went completely.

Carl reached across the table and took Megan's hand. His hand was large and warm. The wounds splitting the calluses were healing, but she could still feel the veil they left across his skin.

"Do I seem mysterious?"

Megan shrugged.

"You had parents; they died. You were a photojournalist, now retired. You loved a woman once; she's gone. What's missing?"

"Certainly you've learned things about me from reading the journals."

"You write objectively about everything, from a description of an exotic bird to a wound you received while cleaning a knife. Did it even hurt?"

"What?"

"Cutting yourself. You never bothered to recall the pain, only the location and depth of the wound."

"Many things have hurt me, Megan, but I have conscious amnesia when it comes to pain, either physical or psychological."

"Is that why the hyacinth woman left you?"

"I told you she left with one of her models."

"Maybe it was because you didn't share your feelings with her. Did you tell her how much it hurt to lose her?"

241

"She knows, Megan. I don't think she understands completely, but she knows."

"Where is she now?"

Carl's smoky eyes were looking beyond Megan.

"Not far away."

"Will you go to her someday?"

He turned back to Megan's face and squeezed her hand between his roughened palms.

"She's no one for you to think about, since you'll take her place."

Megan's body tingled. Did she want to replace such a woman? An awesome task, she pondered, recalling the delicate sketches she had reviewed. Nonetheless, he was presuming. She never said she would stay. Never said she loved him. Never heard him say he loved her.

Megan tried to pull away from his hold, but his hands grew hotter as they held on tighter, a slick film of sweat covering her young skin.

Carl's eyes searched her face. What did he want? Confused, she declared her love. Carl released her and smiled drolly.

"What are you going to do today?" he asked.

Shaken by the sudden turn in the conversation, Megan stared at Carl.

"We could picnic. Yes, why don't we do that? Let's take the boat further upstream, stop at a shady cove, and dine al fresco. Shall we do that?"

A flash of hope sparked in Megan's mind. *Please, Carl, please include me in your private life.*

"I'd like to picnic in the garden behind the yellow house. I'd like to gather some hyacinths to bring back here."

Carl shook his head.

"I don't want you to see the house up close until I've managed to tidy up the place."

"When will you do that?"

"After I've gotten your response to my request that you stay for the winter. Then I'll repair all the loose boards, tighten all the pipes, clean out the furnace, and drive out all the old spooks to make room for my beautiful conquest." He took her right hand and raised the palm to his lips to kiss it. "Since you sit so mutely, I take it for granted you are not going to favor me with an affirmative answer today. Therefore, we should ransack the cupboards and refrigerator for edibles to take on our cruise up the river."

Sullenly, Megan helped Carl. His words kept repeating inside her head. ". . . drive out all the old spooks." Is that how he saw his mother, as someone already dead, who was looming about making a nuisance of herself? Or was Beverly an aged spirit refusing to die? Megan visualized the hand that she had seen yesterday and the blackened chin she had noticed the day before. Megan could almost believe that she had been speaking, touching, communicating with one already deceased. Her disbelief overcame the horror of that proposition. She looked next to her at a man who could be captivating yet mercurial.

The picnic cheered Megan, and she managed to forget Beverly for an afternoon. They coupled under a sweeping weeping willow tree. Megan couldn't call the act love, because Carl held something out of her reach, some sort of bait that lured her in deeper even though she couldn't pronounce what it was.

When they got back to the house, both were exhausted. Megan chose to stay awake for a while. Carl kissed her on the forehead and disappeared into the bedroom. Drowsily, Megan searched the hall closet until she found a flashlight. With flashlight in hand, she walked toward the back door and the crumbling shed. Beverly wanted a shovel; that had to be where Carl would keep things like that.

Dew had settled. Watery brush scraped against the sunburn on her leg, irritating the sensitive nerves.

"Great," she said, looking at the solid door leaning against its hinges.

After putting down the flashlight, Megan grasped the edges of the door and lifted with a strong yank. Her body was jostled by the sudden lightness of the wood. Megan set the door aside, then retrieved her flashlight.

Spiders. Carl had warned her to stay away. Hesitant to enter, Megan flashed the beam around the shed. In the near corner she saw a fat handle emerging above a sooty rag.

"I bet that's a shovel," she whispered, wiggling her nose and consciously stilling her shoulders after a brief shiver.

Her hand reached out, but the shovel wasn't close enough to reach from the doorway. Cringing and with teeth chattering from the damp night and fear, Megan eased her way into the shed, centering all her attention on the handle. One quick grab and she could be gone, but her skittish fumbling dragged on the rag, knocking over a box full of negatives.

She couldn't leave them there. Carl might walk on them, ruining any attempt at making further prints. Although she did wonder how good it was to store negatives in an unheated shed. Still, she was responsible.

Megan shoved the shovel out the door, turned, squatted, and began to right the mess she had made.

When she finished, Megan slid the box back where it had been. As she did, she spied another journal. A well-used journal, coated with dirt and webs, and slime from who knew what. Gingerly she picked it up. She wondered whether Carl knew it was out there or whether it had been misplaced. It absolutely didn't belong in the shed.

With book in hand, Megan left. She would show it to Carl in the morning—not that she expected any sentimental rewards. Carl was miserly with his emotions. That was one thing her father had not been. Until . . . until he became ill. She looked to the house and at the bedroom window. There was no light. Carl had been tired, although he seemed fit. Was he really ill, or was his mother lying? No, Beverly wasn't lying, she believed. Megan assumed Beverly was fantasizing. The woman must have missed her. Too bad she hadn't been able to tell Beverly that she would be there the following day. The shovel would make up for her absence, even if Megan hadn't had a chance to work on the drawing.

The book was laid near the shovel. Megan leaned the door back against its hinges.

While she headed back to the house, exhaustion took over her limbs and she dropped the shovel on the wooden porch. There was a dull thud, not loud enough to awaken Carl, but it awakened Megan to the fact that the shovel had landed a quarter of an inch from her toes. Letting out a soft whistle, Megan stepped back down off the porch and stored the book and shovel under it. Tomorrow she could retrieve them. She dared not take these filthy things into the house, where she was bound to bang and clang them in her sleepy stupor.

Chapter 35
Preparation

Beverly whimpered. "Megan. Megan. Where is my Megan?" Her singsong voice came close to being throttled by the dry, peeling flesh within her throat.

It was nearly noon by the readout on the digital clock in the office. Megan, if she were coming, should have been there by now.

Beverly's booted feet scuttled along the oak floor, making smaller and smaller circles until she was dizzy. Then she leaned against a wall until her sight was clear.

"Megan. Megan. Megan." Occasionally her speech was slurred by a foreign thought that attempted to drive this Megan person from Beverly's consciousness.

Slipping her gloved hand inside the pocket, she touched the matchbook she had found in the depths of one of the kitchen drawers. She pulled the matchbook out, flicking it open with a thumb. Five matches with blue caps were lined up in the back row. Beverly would need only one, but it was good to know that backups existed. Carefully, as if the matchbook were gold, she tucked the cover inside the flap and carefully placed the matches back into her pocket, making sure that it hit the sewn bulge at the bottom. She didn't want it to fall out. Not before the act was completed. She had so little time left.

The girl would bring the drawing. Yes, she would. Of course, she would have to approve it. Beverly concentrated, trying to recall every wrinkle, every mold or freckle, every hair on Carl's body. The contours of his face and body were easy; it was the minute details that she would have to retrieve from her crumbling mind. Scars, birthmarks. *Oh Lord!* She was panicking. *Can't lose control now. Can't forget what to do.* Plans. Made all the plans. Megan must follow through.

"Megan. Megan. Megan." Beverly started to whirl about the room, hitting pieces of furniture, spinning into her madness.

"Megan. Beverly. Megan. Beverly." She heard herself chanting the two names. Were they one person or two?

There was a voice not the same as hers. Higher pitch. Softer tone. No gravel spitting rough chords into letters.

"Beverly?"

"Megan!"

Beverly scurried, as the dead rats at her feet had done when seeking their prey, until she reached the bedroom. At the threshold she tried to calm her emotions, but found her body to be jumpy and jerky.

"Megan," she whispered, shoving her leathered fingertips deep inside the pockets. She pressed her palms against her thighs. If she could only keep herself from flying off into the rage of her excitement.

"Hi, Beverly, are you all right? I was worried when you didn't answer. Didn't you hear me?"

Beverly's body trembled. Megan carried a shovel, a sketch pad, and a dirty old book.

Her limbs shook as she crossed the floor to stand in front of Megan.

"The drawing."

"Sorry, not quite finished yet, but I did remember the shovel. I can dig a hole for the plant."

"Hole? Plant? Where's the drawing?"

"It's only partially completed."

"Let me see." Beverly's hands jumped from the pockets to end up outstretched between the two women.

"You might be disappointed if I let you see it now. Give me another day or two. I wasn't able to do any work on it yesterday—"

"Lazy girl."

Megan was looking down at the pad, refusing to face Beverly.

"Teasing, Megan. I'm teasing you. Yes, that's what I'm doing. Laugh, please laugh. Don't let me make you angry. Don't go away and leave me alone."

"I tried to get Carl to come out and see you, but for some reason he refuses."

Beverly gurgled as the tightness in her throat squished the traveling larvae.

"I didn't tell him I'd met you. I only hinted that he should come to the yellow house and do some repairs."

With a thick cough, Beverly brought up the ground material, spitting the mobile sputum into the folds of her shawl. When she turned her face back to Megan, she noticed that the girl had moved several feet back from her.

"A cold, Megan. Nothing serious."

"I just don't like catching those things during the summer. They're harder to get rid of during the warm months."

"If you don't want to come down with what I have, then work quickly on that drawing, or else you'll be spitting up the bugs." Beverly leaned forward as if to approach Megan, but knew her limitations in the summer sun.

"Believe me, I know how bad a summer bug can be. I guess you're right; it takes more than one to give you a cold, doesn't it?"

Beverly shook her head. The thick, wet portion of her shawl rested against her neck. It cooled the rising ire.

"So where do you want the hole dug?"

"I want the drawing first."

"I'm sure we don't need the drawing of Carl in order to plant a bush or whatever."

"First, the drawing," Beverly reiterated.

"If you insist. I'll put the shovel under the swing. I've got an interesting book here."

"Megan, I don't care about the book. I want the drawing. Stop spending your time making love and reading and do some work."

Beverly was tired of watching the girl blush. *She'll be eighty and blushing at her fiftieth wedding anniversary,* Beverly thought crossly.

Megan turned her back to Beverly, squatted down to slip the shovel under the swing, then rose to place the book and sketch pad on the seat.

So slow. The girl took forever to complete any task, thought Beverly.

"Hurry!" Beverly's body shook. "I can't do it all myself. You must hurry."

"Do what yourself?" Megan's voice was not clear, her back still facing Beverly.

"The hole, the drawing, the fire. So much to do." Beverly coughed up another wad of larvae. She checked to see if Megan was watching before spitting it into the dirt.

"Oh, the roses!" Megan had moved to the right side of the garden. "The leaves are covered with white powder. And look, there are tiny spiders spinning threads between the leaves."

"But the hyacinths are beautiful, aren't they, Megan?"

The hyacinths stood untouched on either side of the rosebushes.

"Yes, they are. Do you have any spray for the fungus on the roses? I could spray them before I leave. Do you think it would help if I trim the bushes?"

"Let them die!" The force of Beverly's breath brought up a mobile force of wiggly creatures. They slid blindly across her tongue and rode the air out between her lips.

Megan knelt near the base of a rosebush. Weeds swarmed around the plant. She turned to look at Beverly, who held her hand up to her mouth.

"It wouldn't take long to care for these plants, but if you'd like, I'll work on the drawing first."

Beverly's head nodded dully, resigned to anything Megan had to say.

Beverly watched Megan set up her things. When the girl appeared settled in her work, Beverly turned back to her own bedroom and started picking up the loose clothes lying about. She pulled a few more items from the drawers and armoire. With a hefty pile of clothing bundled in her arms, Beverly started for the kitchen. Once inside the room, she walked to the center, just under an old hanging Tiffany lamp. She dropped everything that had been in her arms onto the floral linoleum floor.

After making sure all the doors and windows were shut tight, she began to pick up bunches of clothing, which she then used to fill in the cracks and crevices around the windows and back door. The door leading from the hall to the kitchen would have to be done last. She put a small pile of clothes to the side of the entry hall.

Chapter 36
Who Is She?

Carl flipped his sketch pad shut. It was finally finished. That night, he would take a good look at Megan to make sure he hadn't left anything out. He doubted that he had, since he had been working from the nude photographs he had taken of her.

He chuckled, thinking about how lucky he had been these many years. Every time he had needed a new subject, one had arrived under his nose as if the gods blessed his parasitic life.

Carl locked the bottom desk drawer after he had slipped the pad into it. He leaned back in his chair to rest and gloat. Beverly's pervasive presence by way of the hyacinths didn't mean anything anymore. She hadn't been able to prevent him from completing his task. Had she even tried? he wondered. Was that flowery stink just a coincidence? If it was, so what? Long after her remains were gone, he'd probably find a wild bunch of hyacinths growing down near her grave. By then, Megan would be ensconced in the yellow house herself.

Where was she, anyway? Carl realized that she had been quiet all day. What could possibly take up her time? That trashy old journal he had given her to read? She'd never get to see the best volume. Carl had decided not to tell her anything about the transition that would take place. He would care for her as an invalid. Promise her medical help as soon as the doctor got back to town. Of course, there was a small medical clinic in town, but she didn't have to be told about it. He was glad that he hadn't broken down and taken her into town with him. The less she knew about her surroundings, the better.

Carl laughed out loud. Suddenly, looking around the room at nothing but his book-filled bookcases, he quieted. Megan would come scampering if she thought he was in a jovial mood.

It had been so easy with Megan. No one knew about their relationship. No one even knew that they were acquainted. Besides, his feelings for her were not the same as they had been for Beverly. Megan was cute, but he wouldn't miss her very much. He hoped that since she was young her body would last out the winter before he had to bury another image.

Carl stood and walked to the window. He pulled back the nylon curtains, which were backed by a cheap, cream-colored rayon lining. Twilight was looming, bringing some quiet to the backyard. The diurnal creatures were tiring and beginning to retreat. When the sun set, the nocturnal predators would be out stalking in the tall grass.

He let the curtain fall back across the window. Carl supposed that he should look for Megan while his drawing was fresh in his mind. Then he could simply make his mental comparisons and perhaps make some quick alterations if necessary. Usually there were some slight errors. He wasn't even sure if it was necessary to be as precise as he was. Still, he wasn't willing to risk his life on the chance that a missed mole or freckle didn't matter.

Carl ambled to the study door, unlocked and opened it. The interior of the house was dim and quiet. Shadows lurked around the curves of the hall. Opened doorways emphasized the emptiness of the house. He walked to the kitchen to call out Megan's name. He wanted to keep her far away from the study, especially with the completed drawing sitting inside his desk drawer. Carl didn't want a near disaster like what had almost happened with Beverly. Shaking his head, he recalled how he had given her the drawing. Such a fool.

"Megan," he called out again. Damn, was she down by the river? Could she be wandering around looking for the invisible hyacinths? Carl laughed. There was a logical reason for that perfumed stench. There had to be.

Carl stretched his arms out and over his head. He needed some exercise, and it had to be more than the sex play he planned for that evening. Maybe the next day he'd row down to the yellow house to see Beverly once more before he destroyed her shell and took her remains down to the river. He flexed his arms to test the power and tautness of his muscles. Was there a slight limpness? Rechecking, he flexed again. Still tight, no wasting as yet.

"Beverly, you came through, even though initially I wasn't so positive," he declared aloud.

"How did she come through?"

He heard the thin voice and immediately looked away from his bulging shirtsleeve to see Megan standing in the doorway between the hallway and the kitchen.

"I was mumbling things to myself. Don't pay any attention to what I say."

"What about Beverly?"

"A woman I knew in the past. The hyacinth woman."

He watched as Megan's body went rigid.

"Beverly, the hyacinth woman. But you said—"

"It's in the past, Megan. I told you that relationship is long over. She went off with her lover. Here I am with mine." He walked to her and hugged an unresponsive Megan. "What's

257

wrong with you, my love?" He hoped she wasn't going to give him a hard time about having sex before dinner or before dark or whatever other silly excuse she could think up.

"What was your mother's name, Carl?"

"My mother's name. Why would you care? I told you both my parents are deceased."

"She had a name. What was it?"

"I don't like to talk about my family."

"Not even to mention their names? Does this have anything to do with the superstition among the Amazonian tribe?"

"What?"

"You know. There was a tribe you visited that wouldn't speak the name of a dead relative. The person's name was retired, kind of like the number on a football jersey. It was in the journal I just read."

Carl bristled at the analogy, but thought it best to let the subject pass.

"My past isn't what's on my mind right now. No, all I'm thinking about now is seducing you. I've thought about it all day, Megan. Seeing you under me, tasting that mouth." The pads of his fingertips glided lightly across her lips.

Megan's eyes were a drab umber in the dimly lit kitchen. There was no sparkle, no laughter, no desire. He wasn't giving up; the final pass on the drawing would be made that night, not at Megan's leisure.

Carl cupped her cheeks in his palms. Her muscles were straining against her emotions.

Was she fighting her desire, or something else? It didn't matter to Carl, because he would win. He leaned forward to place a kiss on her forehead. Her head tried to pull back, out of his grasp. His hold was firm. When his lips touched her skin, her hands immediately flattened against his chest, pushing. Not shoving; she exerted no great pressure. But she pushed.

He didn't want to ask what was the matter. He didn't want to waste the time. Instead, Carl's lips passed down across Megan's eyelids, he slid his tongue down the bridge of her nose, then he nipped at her upper lip. As she tried to speak, Carl thrust his tongue deep inside her mouth, feeling the muffled sounds hit the nerves of his tongue.

When her hands dropped from his chest, Carl dared to drop his own hands to her body. She didn't pull away. Her arms hung at her sides. Her tongue tried to block his invasion. He looked at her face and saw her eyes squeezed tightly shut. Lines spread out from the viselike closure of the lids. His wandering hands found the two little fists pressed into the outside of her thighs.

His arms enclosed her straight body.

"Relax, Megan," he said. "I'll answer all the questions you want to ask later. I've missed you all day and need to feel close to you. Sometimes you're so distant."

"Me!" she responded, but Carl placed a finger atop her full lips.

"Please, Megan. This house echoes with the loneliness I've experienced. Please, give yourself to me. I need to be warmed by you, even if we just lie together on the bed. Take away my pain for the short time you're here. Please, Megan." He breathed her name into her ear, blowing aside a stray curl. The flesh of his arms vibrated with the shiver that shook her body. She pulled her head back, then laid it on his shoulder as they passed through the doorway on their way to the bedroom.

Chapter 37
Discovery

Lie with her. All the man wanted to do was get laid. Once that was done, he rushed back to the study to finish more work. What the hell was he working on, his own version of *War and Peace*? Megan asked herself. She had no answers, only questions.

Ah, yes! He promised to answer any and all that she presented to him, but how could she even ask him what was for dinner without banging on that blasted door?

Megan rolled over onto her stomach and began to kick the mattress, using her fists to jab rights and lefts into the pillow usually used by Carl. Her limbs suddenly relaxed, and her body exploded into silent sobs. Tears wet the sheet while her nose stuffed up, forcing her to regain her self-control. She rolled over and looked around the room for a tissue. Finding none, Megan spitefully blew as hard as she could into the edge of the pillowcase on which her head rested.

"Stupid, perverse man," she gritted out.

She had been happy that afternoon. Before leaving Beverly's, whoever the damn woman was, Megan had been able to place the final draft of the drawing of Carl on the floor of the bedroom. She hadn't wanted to disturb Beverly. Possibly she was resting. Besides, she had seemed rather cranky that day. What if the drawing hadn't been up to snuff? Better to let Beverly find it later, after Megan had left. Beverly could complain later, if she wanted, but Megan's real hope was that the woman would be delighted and spend a comforted night staring at her son's image. If he was her son. Certainly Beverly didn't look like anyone Carl had dated or knew in the biblical sense, although he had proclaimed Beverly the hyacinth woman. That couldn't be. She was confused. Perhaps he loved Beverly, if she was his mother. Or, at least, Megan wanted to believe he loved her. But she couldn't forget the stench that emanated from that house. Megan almost retreated several times before her arm's-length reach could drop the drawing onto the wood floor of the bedroom. Was it the woman's disease, she wondered, or plain old filth? Carl wasn't the best housekeeper; he wasn't even in the running for a passable housekeeper, but there weren't any highly offensive odors trapped in dead air in his house.

That's what the air was, dead, Megan recalled. Exactly. It was as if the woman were keeping her own private morgue, with bodies lying about unrefrigerated. Megan twitched her nose, recalling the dense smell.

"Maybe I could clean the house up for her or help her bathe," Megan whispered. No, she wasn't the domestic type, nor the nursing type. She'd keep her good deeds confined to the garden. "And who the hell is Beverly, anyway?" This was said in a louder voice. Megan didn't care whether Carl heard her. Evidently he hadn't, she figured after several minutes, since there was no response.

She glanced over at the shut window. Carl had fixed the windowpane the day he brought the replacement glass home. For a man who had gotten used to the smell of hyacinth, it was strange how he still kept that window shut and locked.

Megan bounded out of bed, heading straight for the window. She snapped the lock, then pulled the frame open. A gush of hyacinth sprang into the room. It was almost as if the flower had been pressing up against the glass, waiting for any opportunity to enter the bedroom.

Standing tall, Megan sucked the sweet fragrance up through her nostrils, filling her lungs, then exhaled it with a refreshed sigh.

She wasn't going to worry about his weird idiosyncrasies anymore. It was time he did a bit of catering to her.

After pulling a gray, short-sleeved sweatshirt over her head, she picked her jeans up off the floor and slipped into them. She got on her hands and knees and crawled under the bed, brushing dust bunnies away with flicks of her hands until she located her moccasins. They were a bit bent and out of shape, but they were the most comfortable things she could think of sticking her feet into at the moment.

Megan stood, marched to the bedroom door, and flung it open. Carl had gently closed it about forty-five minutes earlier. He had obviously believed that she was going to fall asleep.

When she reached the door to Carl's study, she turned to face it squarely. Her mouth was a straight line, the skin on her face tight, the brows low over her eyelids. Megan raised her right fist and hit the door.

"Yes?" Carl answered calmly.

Megan repeated the blow.

"What is it, Megan?"

Again she pounded the door, except this time she repeated the effort twice.

The lock turned. Carl opened the door two inches.

"Did you want something?" He appeared in no way perturbed.

Megan screamed, then grabbed the doorknob. She slammed the door shut in her own face, and screamed again. Megan heard the lock slip back into place.

"Idiot," she yelled.

Her feet traveled the wooden floor with heavy thuds. By the time she reached the living room, she was pouty and her eyes were clouding with tears.

"I don't understand you, Carl. I don't understand you," she softly whimpered.

Through the watery glaze of her eyes, she managed to make out the form of the journal she had wanted to return to Carl. The one she had found in the shed. It was lying on the sofa, where she had left it after she had returned from Beverly's.

She retrieved a flashlight from the hall closet, lifted the journal from the sofa, and went out onto the front porch. There she found an old chair whose wicker seat was becoming unraveled. There was nothing else to sit on except the splintery front steps before her. Deciding the river would have more atmosphere, she descended the steps and intended to continue down the path to the river, but midway the hyacinths lured her into the tall grass.

The dried mound seemed to shimmer under the moonlight. A worm was busy burying itself into the highest peak. In the dark it looked so much like a grave, thought Megan. She switched on the flashlight, and the worm disappeared completely. Megan fanned the light in a semicircle around her. She thought she saw the leaves of a bush shiver, but saw nothing else move. There wasn't anything there but dry earth and blossomless plants starving for attention, just like her. This was comfortable, she decided, and settled her behind on a cleared piece of earth beside the mound. She rested the flashlight just below shoulder level on a rock on her other side. Atop her slightly bent knees she laid the battered journal, giving her the best advantage of the battery-powered light.

The cover of the journal fell back as she opened it, almost pulling completely free from the gluing of the threadlike spine.

"Maybe this will give me insight into how your mind works," she whispered. However, she had already run through three of his earlier journals and had come away with nothing but objective facts. "It's worth another try."

The first page offered the date, the time, descriptions of the flora, and pertinent information about the fishing. Pollution from the mercury used by gold miners had caused a severe population decrease of the pirarucu fish, which he had annotated was once an Amazonian staple. A sad note on what civilization can bring, but Megan wanted information about the man writing these words. Did he care about the environment? Or was he just recording facts for a possible book when he returned to his own intrusive world?

Megan flipped through several more pages, searching for a personal observation, or an emotion, that might have escaped through the tip of his pen.

She was practically near the end of the journal when the pages became blurred. Ink streaked from letters, and words dripped down across the tidy blue lines. Pages carried the creases of rough fingertips. The corners of several of the pages had been turned down, marking them as significant. Megan turned back to the beginning of that section and began to read each word aloud.

Chapter 38
The Amazon

September 15

Since I've learned the Indians' language and have been able to dispense with the awkward grunts, grimaces, and gesticulations. I have gathered a good deal of information about the beliefs of this tribal people. They do not hoard; instead, they share everything, from space in one of their sleeping hammocks to the food and beverage, which sometimes runs low. If they must move on to find additional prey for food, it is simple for them to pack up their belongings and chop down the poles that support the great palm fronds that offer them shelter.

Currently, I am living in the headman's hut and sleeping regularly with two of his daughters. Although the Indians appear to be mainly mo-

nogamous, they occasionally allow an honored person to bed more than one woman. Since they are grateful for the cheap trinkets I have brought with me, I fall into the category of an honored guest.

The headman's mother died this morning, and I have been told by one of my paramours that there will be a big feast tonight to send the old woman off in style. She had been a rather grumpy, scrawny woman with a withered leg, and I personally will not miss her. I would have expected a number of the young hunters to have left the village to search for food, but it seems no one has bothered. Perhaps, in the tradition of most religions, we will fast in atonement for her caustic personality.

I am still not used to the number of insects that come out following the afternoon rain showers. The mosquitoes and the chicharra are a special problem for me. Often I must dig out the eggs of some of these insects from under my skin to prevent a deeper parasitic invasion.

I have just remembered that I should seek out my friend and guide Tutirahi before the festivity begins. He has promised to teach me the use of the twenty-five-foot blowgun I admired the other day.

September 16

Fortunately, before the ceremony my women introduced me to ebene, a narcotic snuff, which we blew into one another's nostrils; otherwise, I don't believe I could have made it through the so-called meal. Yesterday, in the early evening, I smelled meat roasting. Thinking that they had captured some game while I was getting high, I happily eschewed a before-dinner bite of pulverized fish. However, when I looked at the night's meal, it looked sadly familiar with its foreshortened limb.

In the six months that I have been here, there have been no other deaths. I began to think that mine would be the first to bring about the mourning chants until the headman's mother sickened and quickly deteriorated. That was who had been placed before us for dinner, roasted and oddly silent, considering who it was. I quickly shook my head when my women offered me the choice bits, which included a slice of the pinkish heart. I had gotten used to the fact that most of the prepared meat was semi-raw, but this I could not stomach. The only missing part was the head, which I was told was being set aside until it filled up with maggots. Then it would be spiced with herbs before eating.

The headman, who was decked out with his ceremonial leg ligatures and the red paint from annatto seeds, attempted to sway me into partaking with my fellow brothers. This experience would qualify me as a full-fledged member of the tribe, he assured me. As much as I have tried to be accepted, I could not go that far. It was bad enough to eat another human being's flesh, but to add the fact that it was the tedious bitch who had made so many lives miserable . . .

His eldest daughter brought me some fish that had been heated over hot coals for storage for the rainy season when game was scarce. I attempted to chew on the fish to show how grateful I was for her effort, but it constantly caught in the back of my throat.

Later, while the Indians danced. I was able to withdraw to a quiet section of the forest where there were only the sounds of my own breathing and the hoarse call of the bullfrogs.

September 19

I have not written in several days. My illness has gotten worse, and I am afraid that soon it will start to affect my neurological system; then I will be unable to hold a pen steady in my hand. If only the headman's daughters had taken my efforts to teach them my language more seriously, then they could have continued this journal up until the day of my death. But who will there be to read it, anyway? Will I, too, be gobbled up by my friends, or will they consider me too much of an outsider to taint their bodies? I am afraid to ask, just as I am afraid to admit my illness to anyone here.

Perhaps I should speak with the headman. I do not want my friends in the tribe to fear me once the disease takes hold. I must explain it completely to the headman this night.

September 20

    Can I believe him? The headman insists that he would have been dead many years ago, except for the ritual he follows when he feels his own strength being sapped away.

    He had received a wound that had become infected, and most thought he would die. However, a prominent shaman shared his own secret with the valued headman. First, the headman must capture a victim from an enemy village. Second, he must with his own hands carve an exact replica of that captured person. Third, he must bury it deep in the soil. No words need be spoken, no hocus-pocus of ritualistic dancing or hand waving. All that was needed was intent and a strong will to transfer his own death to another.

    I asked why he had not saved his mother this way. He smiled at me, his teeth strong and white, and said that he had no desire to save the crone. The privilege was reserved for an elite few. Think what the population would be, he thought with a chuckled, if everyone had the knowledge.

    He was right, but how could this information save me? I asked. For one thing, wood carving was not a strong point with me. He interrupted to clarify that it need not be a carved statue; a drawing could serve the same purpose. Accuracy was the important ingredient.

    I nodded and acknowledged that I had studied art back home, but—He cut me off and reminded me that another important aspect was my desire to perform the impartation.

As I sit here near the night's fire and listen to the twigs crackle and twist, flinging themselves deeper into the flames. I want to believe. I want my life back. I don't want to have to fear death and the decay that follows. Now I even find myself praying to a God that I do not believe exists. Odd how religion comes to bulwark us in times of stress.

Truly, I know my days are few and that nothing but oblivion awaits me.

September 23

The headman called me to the edge of the village this afternoon. His trusted guards held a thin male, who could not have been more than fifteen years old. The youth pulled and tugged, but could do nothing under the strong grasp of the older men.

"He is for you," the headman quietly said.

I shook my head. What would I want with this scared child?

The guards immediately stripped the boy of the meager breechcloth he wore. He had a long scar from his groin to his navel, possibly from a secret tribal ritual he had undergone when he achieved manhood. The headman ran his fingers up and down it, indicating to me that it was important. The boy's penis became aroused and stood in defiance of the four men surrounding him.

"Your paper, your pen, where are they?"

I answered the headman by reaching inside my shirt and pulling out a ratty pad. The pen was *secured to the breast pocket of my shirt.*

"It must be flawless," he reminded, directing the men to spread the boy's arms while he tied the victim to the two trees crowding us on either side.

Although I understood what he wanted, I don't think the guards had a clue as to why I needed a drawing of such a nondescript adolescent.

The headman left me with the guards and my redemption. Strangely, I didn't feel foolish once I started to sketch. I worked as hard on that drawing as on any piece of work I've ever completed. Why not? The boy was going to rescue me from death.

Later, following the headman's instructions, I buried the drawing deep in the ground so that the rains would not flush it up. The guards released the prisoner. He returned, visibly unharmed, to his village.

"What will happen to the boy?" I asked the headman before retiring with his youngest daughter.

"He will rot into the earth" was his simple reply.

September 30

It is working, I'm sure of it. I must have had enough belief after all. My skin is no longer pallid under my tan; my muscles are again firming up. All the symptoms I had described earlier in this journal are retreating. Strength returns each minute. I will live.

Chapter 39
Truth

"What the hell are you doing?"

The journal slipped between Megan's bent knees and fell to the ground. Instantly, Megan stood, her hand grasping for the flashlight on the rock next to her. By the time she had it firmly in her hand, Carl had moved in closer. The beam of light flashed into his face, forcing him to shut his eyes. Carl extended his arm out in front of him.

"Shut that damn thing off."

Megan swiftly lowered the beam, so that Carl's naked feet glowed in the night.

"What are you doing out here, Megan?"

She could barely make out his features, but what she could see looked angry. His voice railed on about how she shouldn't be wandering off the path in the dark; besides, what did she expect to find here? Through it all Megan was silent.

"What is wrong with you, standing there like an idiot? Come."

Carl reached out to take her arm, but Megan pulled away and felt her foot sink deeper into the loose soil.

"Get off of that!" Carl lunged forward to grab her.

Megan leaned backward, but her feet didn't seem able to move with the rest of her body. It was as if they were stuck in mud or quicksand. She fell, her back hitting the dirt with a thud, and felt a faint shock of a burning pain racing down her spine. The earth was soft, almost muddy. What was happening? she wondered. The aroma of hyacinths intensified. Her hands were filled with dry dirt. Small, pink worms wiggled through the spaces between her fingers.

"Get up!" She heard his voice over her, demanding, scared. "Get up! For God's sake, help yourself."

Her right foot was wedged in the earth; her elbows dug grooves in the earth's slippage. Her skin crawled as if vermin fed on the scaling debris of her flesh.

She felt a jolt on her right arm. The socket ached. Her hands started clawing at air instead of dirt as she was lifted up and carried from the grave. Megan shivered, for she knew now why it smelled so sweet over that mound.

In rapid succession, she registered the firm

mattress beneath her, her moccasins being
yanked off, her clothes pulled from her, and
then the cool sheets under the weight of her
body. Carl pulled the top sheet up to her shoulders. She could see him move over her. He left.
He returned with a glass. Water.

"Here, drink some water."

Megan stared at his face. The tan, aged wrinkles, the clear blue eyes.

"Drink." He placed the glass at her lips and
threateningly tipped the glass. Either drink or
he will spill it all over you, she told herself. And
the water slid down her chin. Drops fell on the
rounded bones protruding beneath her neck.

The glass and Carl disappeared. Megan
looked toward the window. Moving slowly, as
she started to relearn how to use her body, she
inched her way to the edge of the bed. Her
sheet-covered arms reached up into the air. The
beige sheet skimmed the surface of her forearms as it slowly floated down. Megan reached
out toward the window when one of her legs fell
heavily from the bed to the floor. Soon she
stood. She walked. But before she could throw
open the window, Carl's arms were wrapped
around her, gradually lowering her arms to her
side.

"Come back to bed, Megan. You had a fright,
but it was only a trick of the light."

Liar. *Liar,* she barked out silently through
dusky eyes that wouldn't leave the window.
Liar, she called him numbly inside her head.

He placed a cool towel on her forehead, then again pulled the top sheet over her body.

"Stay here. I'll get you a blanket."

Megan's body rigidly awaited his return.

Then he was back, clutching an old, tightly woven olive-green blanket, spreading it across the beige sheet.

She thought about what lousy taste he had.

"Comfortable?" He smiled, and his teeth glowered at her. "Can I get you anything? Maybe some wine? Or I could squeeze some of your favorite orange juice?" He kissed her fingertips. "Sorry I startled you. I was worried about you when I couldn't find you in the house. I suspected that you might have gone down to the river, so I decided to join you. Midway along the path I heard some muttering, and then I saw the light among the bushes. Forgive me, Megan. Honestly, I was worried."

About whom was he worried? she wondered. Was he afraid of losing his new victim? That's what she was, wasn't she? Sketched-out faces, trunks, and limbs floated across her vision. Two boxes full of drawings. How many hadn't he kept?

His hands were hot; she knew hers were icy. He tried rubbing her fingers; he blew his foul breath on them. Her hands tried to jerk back, but he held fast.

So many women boxed away to die. But he had to have buried a complete drawing in order to survive. The sketches she had found were only drafts, first tries at murder.

"I'm going to make you some hot tea. I want you to stay put. Understand?"

Now I do, she thought.

He hesitated, but she could see that he could think of nothing else to bring her around except hot tea.

"I'll be right back." He patted the blanket, completely missing any portion of her body.

One thought led to another inside her head. Obviously she was his next substitute. Had he already drawn her? The photographs; *my God, the photographs!* Wait, it had to be by his own hand. Certainly he could have drawn her accurately, between their love play and the photographs. Could he already have buried her figure? He didn't seem to be ill yet; perhaps the other person was still rescuing him. Beverly, she must see Beverly; the woman might know something about this. Wait! Beverly had the drawing of Carl. It had to be exact. Was Beverly trying to use the trick on him?

Everything stopped when she felt Carl's arm slip under her head as he brought a steaming cup of tea to her lips. The warmth of the cup soothed her lips open, and she gulped down the liquid, burning the roof of her mouth as she did.

"That's good, Megan. Take some more."

By the time she had finished the tea, a warmth was spreading from her tummy out to the rest of her trunk, returning a tepid sensation to her limbs.

She must be crazy to believe what was in

Carl's journal. There had to be a logical explanation. He probably had some cure, or perhaps his disease was in remission. Megan refused to give credence to a tribal superstition.

"Feeling better?" Carl asked as he fluffed the pillow beneath her head.

Like taut rubber bands, her lips stretched into a smile. No sense asking him about the journal now. First, she would see Beverly, ask about her son's, or whoever's, illness. Why would he have lied about his mother?

Solicitously, Carl began to tuck the ends of the blanket under the mattress. He smoothed the edge neatly, wiping away the thick creases.

"Thank you, Carl." Her voice was feeble, but Carl, alert for anything she might say, immediately grinned at her, his even teeth barely visible.

"You're better?"

Megan nodded.

"Good. Please don't go wandering around at night by yourself. Sometimes I know I'm distracted, not attentive enough, but give me a chance and I'll be there for you."

"Will you?"

"Of course." The laugh lines around his mouth seemed to shiver uncomfortably.

Was he telling her the truth? Had he ever?

Carl bent over and kissed her on the forehead.

"I'm going to turn out the light so you can get some sleep. I'll be in the study if you need me." He was closing the door when he added, "Don't open the window. You're liable to catch a chill after the fright you had." He closed the door softly.

In the dark, Megan's faith in Carl was rocked again by the sketches. And who was Beverly? A part of Megan believed his mother had died many years ago. Another part was calmed by the hope that Beverly was his mother.

Chapter 40
A Gift

Beverly held the drawing of Carl between her leather-gloved fingertips. It was perfect. She herself could never have done such a superb job. The child had artistic talent. Lord knows she would need it. Afraid to lay the paper down anywhere, Beverly walked from room to room with it almost floating between the dark edges of her digits.

"Humpty-Dumpty sat on a wall. Humpty-Dumpty had a great fall." Her fingers teased the paper with her light touch. She was tempted to let the paper fall to the floor, but what if it should get damaged? The child might not be able to duplicate it fast enough. It had taken her a very long time to produce this masterpiece. Oh, it was so perfect. She could visualize the tiny lines around Carl's eyes spreading as he smiled.

Room to room she went. The bedroom French doors were fastened shut. No late-night crawlers there. The kitchen nooks and crevices where air entered were muffled tightly against the evening draft. The bathroom was still splattered ugly, like the hall, but the office was quiet, with a wide, empty expanse across the top of her desk.

Holding the drawing by one edge, Beverly used a portion of her shawl to dust off the top of the desk. Gently she lowered the drawing down onto the surface. Beverly's youthful giggle belied the reflection in the monitor on the worktable. Souring as she glanced in the direction of the computer, Beverly readjusted the shawl over her head.

"Mustn't let Miss . . ." The name; why was she always forgetting the name? "Megan! Yes, mustn't let Miss Megan see me without my coverings. It might frighten her away." Another giggle jiggled her decaying body.

Her leather-covered hand reached inside her pocket to make sure the book of matches was still there. She took the book out, opened the cover, and counted the small sticks once again. Carefully she checked the blue caps to make sure they were strikeable. Nothing would go wrong. She would be ready. After closing the cover, she slipped the book back into her pocket and retreated to the kitchen.

Beverly opened the drawer closest to the sink and saw five knives, their handles raised high by the wooden holder in which they were resting. Her fingers skimmed the handles. One was way too small, another too unwieldy; another was only a serrated bread knife, another a butcher's knife—way too dramatic. Ah, but the one lying under the gloved palm was just right. Beverly dragged the knife out of its slot. Heft was fine. She would have no problem using this one, but was it sharp enough? After flicking on the kitchen light, Beverly began twisting her wrist to check the blade's gleam. Dull. Way too dull, like the brain of that . . . The name wouldn't come to her. "Silly child," she pronounced out loud.

Her booted feet scraped across the linoleum as she returned to the drawer. Where was the sharpening stone? She hadn't used it in a long time. As a matter of fact, she hadn't remembered using it in all the time she had lived there.

Beverly brushed aside a number of corks, some purplish from the wine they had protected in the bottle. Rubber bands way past their usefulness were congealed to the red plaid contact paper lining the bottom of the drawer. Coupons for food items she would never again taste were ripped by her rough, jerky movements.

"Think, Beverly," she whispered. "Slow down and think." Her body, motionless, paused in a frozen pose, her hand lingering over the now useless drawer. "You had it, Beverly, when you moved here. Remember, you took it out of the box. The big box with the silverware and the old rusty iron frying pan."

Beverly swung around and rushed over to the tall cabinet at the far end of the room. She twisted the handle and the door sprung open. A rusty frying pan lay on the top shelf, abandoned. She pulled it down, but there were only a few coffee filters inside. The pot smashed to the floor.

"Think, think, think." Beverly tossed the handle of the knife back and forth between her two hands. "Think, think, think." Was there something else she could use? "No! Think, think, think."

Suddenly her hands clapped, almost making her lose her hold on the knife. She ran into the office, stood at the computer table, and rifled under several old newspapers until she found the stone. Beverly had used it as a paperweight. How could she have forgotten? She lifted the stone up and returned to the kitchen, where, over the sink, she began brushing the blade of the knife across the stone.

When she was finished, tiny metal splinters were scattered across the bottom of the white porcelain sink. Beverly found a piece of paper, which she sliced at with the knife.

"Perfect. As perfect as that girl's creation."

Where could she keep it? Beverly tucked it inside the cord around her waist.

"A sheath. A scabbard. That's what I need," she cheered, spitting fragments of chewed larvae into the air.

Proudly, she wore the blade as she marched through the rooms until she faced the bedroom mirror. Ridiculous, that was how she looked.

"Mmmmmegan." She stuttered the word out, unsure if it was the correct name. "Mmmmmegan wouldn't approve. Frighten Miss Mmmmegan away. She'd run off with the spider by the light of the moon."

Beverly untied the knot on her sash. The knife fell to the floor, narrowly missing the tip of her black leather boot.

"Ruin the point," she cried, quickly scooping up the knife. But the knife looked unharmed. The edge was sharp and the point straight.

She looked around the room for a hiding place. A place where she would be able to retrieve it with little effort.

The bed was bare, and she was afraid to put the knife under the mattress because it might get caught in the coils of the spring. Opening and closing a drawer might take too much time, and sometimes the drawers stuck and squeaked. She needed a simple, unobtrusive place.

Slowly she started to work the knife up her sleeve, point first. She barely felt the coldness of the steel; occasionally a live nerve would jolt to attention and warn her of the hint of the icy metal. But on the whole, it seemed the knife could rest upon the disintegrating flesh without discomfort.

This was no good, though. If the knife had nothing on which it could fasten, it might slip down below the end of the sleeve and become visible or, worse, fall to the ground.

Beverly slanted the knife so that the point faced inward against the skin. On her upper arm there was not much flesh left, but there were still remnants of a strong muscle. An impulsive, heavy-handed shove drove the blade into the muscle. There was little pain. She was surprised. It had been like getting a shot from the doctor, an immediate burn, then numbness. She patted down the sleeve. No major bulge. This would work. It all would work. Beverly wrapped the robe around her body and cinched the sash.

On her way back to the kitchen, she went through her mental checklist. She should have written it all down; she would have been more confident if she had written it all down. What if she forgot a small item? It would ruin everything, and then he would find out and come for her. Beverly shivered, thinking about the river lying in wait just a short walk from her door.

"I'll cheat it." Her voice was a whisper. No need to hex her plan by flouting nature.

In the kitchen she went right to the stove, opening the door to the oven with a handle that dangled downward. She put out the pilot light and turned on all the knobs, releasing the gas at full force. There was the steady whish buzzing in her ears. It took a while for the odor to penetrate her withered senses, but when it did she was joyous.

One last sweep of the room with her eyes, then she retreated to the hallway, where she closed the door and spread the bundled clothes she had waiting across the threshold. Sighing, she turned and continued down the hall to the bedroom. Once there, Beverly sat on the mattress ticking, facing the French doors. She had many hours to wait before . . . She stuttered again, then caught her tongue between her teeth so sharply that the wasted tip fell off.

"Megan," she lisped out. "Megan is coming to dig."

Through the filmy curtains, Beverly was able to see the garden swing, and she knew that under it there lay a shovel. Carl's shovel. How appropriate, she thought. Perhaps it was the same one he had used for her burial. She giggled, and the dried, bitter, flattened end of her tongue pressed against what remained of her teeth.

Chapter 41
Intent

Megan couldn't sleep, and Carl never came to bed. At dawn, Megan got out of bed, found the clothes Carl had removed from her the night before, and put them on. In the bathroom Megan splashed cold water on her face, using a corner of the bath towel to dry off.

She wasn't hungry. There was no need to stop at the kitchen, and the door to the study was closed. Carl never had a chance to see her slip by on her way out.

Her eyes hardly blinked as her feet worked their way down to the middle of the path and then into the shrubbery, kicking around until she made contact with the journal. Bending down, Megan picked up the journal, stood, and continued on her way to the rowboat.

After seating herself inside the small boat,

Megan rowed out into the middle of the river, laid the oars flat on the bottom of the vessel, and reread the last journal entry. The sun was full in the sky before she again lifted her head and saw that she had drifted downriver. Down to the yellow house. Down to Beverly.

Upon landing, Megan flipped the boat over. Clouds were beginning to darken the sky, and she didn't want the boat to fill with rainwater. Carl had told her that showers frequently came on heavily during the summer months, although they never lasted more than a few hours. The water-soaked wood was dark with a webbing of drips drifting down the sides. She had hidden the oars under the boat. She didn't know why. She experienced the quivery chill of danger. Was it directed at her or someone else? And what was the danger? What harm could occur in these docile woods?

Megan walked up to the house, the journal tucked under one arm. She saw that there was a light shining inside the house. The sky had darkened. When she looked up, she saw a blackness covering the sky to her left. It slinked along, creeping up on what sun was trying to radiate through the white clouds. It would definitely rain, and there was no place that offered cover except the house. Would she finally be driven inside that morgue? The porch was hooded by some cheap, painted boards; she imagined the innumerable cracks that chinked its surface. Briefly she thought about climbing the porch steps and ringing the bell like a normal neighbor, but she wasn't visiting a normal friend. She wasn't even sure that Beverly was a friend.

Megan's steps paced their way to the side of the house, where the garden gate stood closed. Her hand unlatched the catch, and she walked in, swinging the gate closed behind her.

The French doors were shut. Beverly wouldn't have expected her so early. The shovel was still beneath the swing. The hyacinths and roses bloomed together in a merry clash of colors. Her gaze went back to the French doors, reminding her that the drawing of Carl might still lie just beyond the threshold. Should she knock? Would Beverly still be sleeping? Probably not, she thought as she recalled the light that had been shining from the front room of the house. Megan knew she was procrastinating. She needed to read the excerpt from the journal once more.

She sat on the swing. The elm's branches above her would offer less protection from the rain than the cheap, painted pine shading the porch; still, this was where she felt the most comfortable, not far from the heavy scent of the hyacinths.

As she read, her stomach began a low rumble, seemingly unconcerned about the anxiety building within her mind. Once she moved her foot, hitting the shovel and stinging her toe.

"Was it really a success, Carl?" Or had Carl's

own mind and determination worked a miracle?

Megan shifted on the seat, uncomfortable. She closed the book and placed it beside the shovel under the swing. That should give it some protection from the rain, she thought.

When she looked straight ahead, she saw movement against the curtains of the French doors. Undoubtedly, Beverly was peeking out at her. Megan wouldn't move. Beverly would have to come for her.

Quickly the doors were parted and the clownish ghost stood proudly at the threshold. No drawing at her feet. Obviously Beverly had found the sheet with Carl's naked image stretched across it.

"Mmmmegan," the black shawl seemed to stutter at her. There was no hint of a face, so how could there be lips? "Mmmmegan, come here, girl."

"I'm not a girl."

"Sorry." The mask giggled. "I have a request to make. That shovel." The black-gloved hand waved spastically. "Pick it up."

"Why?"

"I . . . I have a plant. A big plant, really a small tree. I need you to dig a hole for it. It must be buried today. There isn't much time left."

No, Megan thought, *this is not Carl's mother. This is one of the women with the unconnected limbs contained within the sketch pads, boxed away inside that closet. This is the hyacinth girl.*

Megan bent over and lifted the shovel. It was not very heavy. She stood.

"Where do you want me to dig, Beverly?"

"Anywhere. There." Beverly pointed to a spot that was heavily shaded by hyacinth plants.

Megan approached the spot. She struck the ground with a violent push. The dirt loosened easily, filling the spade with brown earth and green grass. She kept digging.

"Make it wider, Mmmegan. Wider."

Big enough for an eleven-by-seventeen sheet, Megan thought. She dug the hole broader. Broader and deeper.

It grew darker. One would have mistaken it for twilight, but Megan knew it couldn't be more than nine A.M. when she turned to Beverly.

"Is that enough?"

"Widen it, Mmmegan. Make it big enough so that you can fit inside, and deepen it."

"I think I need a rest."

"Not too long. We must finish. It's going to rain. Must be completed before the rain."

Yes, thought Megan, the rain could cause the drawing to run; it would mar its perfection. Megan hefted the shovel up, and with aching arms she began again.

By noon it was wide enough and deep enough, and Megan was stiff enough to have a great deal of difficulty climbing out of the hole.

"Quickly, you clumsy girl. Quickly!"

"Who are you, Beverly?" breathed Megan as

her body rose up and out of the mouth of the grave.

"Me? I'm Beverly," she said with a giggle. "You're Mmmegan. See, I remember."

"How are you related to Carl?"

"Related? I'm his ghost. Yes, that's what I am. His spirit, suffering the tortures of a hideously long death."

"You were one of his lovers, weren't you?"

Beverly came out of the house, moving toward Megan. The sky was almost black with the watery weight of the clouds. Megan squatted next to the grave, for she no longer had any doubt about what she had been digging. Carl's final home, but he would never rest in peace there under the pungent scent of the hyacinths. Megan didn't care.

Beverly stood inches from Megan, forcing her to slip from a squat to a sitting position. Beverly bent down toward Megan. The shawl-covered head slowly shook back and forth.

"Who are you, then?"

Megan watched Beverly's right hand reach inside the left sleeve. She saw the leather glove jerk in a strong yank, but Megan was blinded by the shock of the blade appearing from out of the sleeve.

"I'm his murderer!" Beverly screamed as she stabbed down into Megan's chest.

"No!" Megan cried; then she felt the cold steel slide back out. Again she saw the knife plunge down, the pain leaving her breathless for a second. The knife was free again and held high. Beyond the blade, she saw Death, a mottled scab of dripping flesh with sockets loosely holding the brown jelly orbs. The shawl fell off of a bald pate that was covered with opened sores. Maggots dropped from widely flared nostrils. The blade fell; Megan was almost beyond the pain. Death had come personally for her, and she saw it use a short, gristled tongue to lap at the dangling skin on its lips, sucking up the purplish, chapped flesh with one last powerful lick.

Megan fell back on the ground. She was alone. The sky, on the verge of tears, muffled the lightning that hit in the distance.

Death was back with its clownish garb, rolling Megan over toward the grave. She thought that she was about to be dropped in when the drawing was placed in her hands. Megan took it. Death stretched Megan's elbows out, so that her hands hung above the grave. Megan let go of the drawing. She couldn't see it fall, because Death had already started putting clumps of earth in her fists.

"Throw it in, child. Hurry!"

Megan sprinkled a few handfuls, but was too weak to close her hand anymore.

"Push, then, Mmmegan. Push!"

Her hands fell on the loose soil and tried to brush it back into the grave.

"You've covered the drawing, Mmmegan. That will have to do. I'll finish."

Death picked up the shovel and scooped the

earth up, throwing back into the hole what Megan had dug up. Megan winced as she tried to roll away from the bizarre tableau. Eventually she lay still, staring at the sky, waiting to be washed away into the dirt.

Death was finished. It knelt next to her. She smelled the fetid breath, a mingling of vermin and rot. That's how she would smell.

"Relax, Mmmegan. I have taken care of everything. Rest."

"The jour—" Megan started to say, but Death placed two black leather fingers on her lips.

"I must go. I can't be here when he finds out what I've done." Death giggled like a child, giggled with a raspy hoarseness that denied its youth.

The fingers left Megan's lips and reached inside the pocket of the robe. Megan saw it pull something out of its pocket. Matches. Death was delighted and returned to the house, leaving Megan alone.

Nature stood silenced by the scene. Megan began to cry in the solitude of her demise. She never had wanted to die alone. She never considered Death to be so close.

A roar in her ears. A clap of thunder before the storm?

Grayish-black smoke rose into the sky. The smell of burning debris. Painfully, Megan raised her head. The house was burning.

My God, she thought, *I am absolutely alone.* Even Death had abandoned her.

What had the journal said? Intent was what was most important. The desire for the impartation to take place.

"Carl, you bastard!" Her voice cried out beneath the tumble of raindrops and the rumble of the storm.

Chapter 42
Don't Let Me Die

Megan closed her eyes to the rain that was
splattering her prone body. She felt the chill of
her wet clothes burn her chest wounds, but she
couldn't rise up to take cover. Where was the
white light that was supposed to lead her to the
next world? All she saw was the blackness of her
rain-soaked eyelids. She squinted as a few of the
drops managed to glide underneath the lids.
Her chest ached with such pain that she held
her breath several times. Where was the white
light? Where was the peace of the next world?
Megan didn't want to die, and she exalted in the
shiver shaking her body, an acknowledgment of
her still being alive.

A strong wind whipped across her body. Her
clothes felt like a second skin, clinging to her
against the elements. She started to scream out

her anguish but stopped when the pain tore through her chest, sending out fingerlike waves of torture throughout her trunk, subsiding gradually into her limbs. She kept her mouth open, swallowing down big gulps of water. Gradually she raised her mouth up toward the water, capturing more of the liquid that her parched mouth craved, almost drowning herself in the rain that tumbled down into her nostrils and thus into her lungs. Convulsive coughing followed. Her chest seemed to crumple in upon the pain.

Eventually Megan stilled her freezing body. Her temperature must be way below normal, she contemplated. If she didn't die from the loss of blood, she would die of shock. No, she was going to survive. Using shallow breaths, Megan concentrated on transferring her death to the grave beside which she lay. To the grave and to the drawing. She visualized the figure of Carl. The blond hair with the sparks of gray that always captured the light indoors or out. His face, the wrinkles around the eyes, the prominent straight nose, and the swelling lips underneath. Ah, and his body tanned and hairy, the muscles contoured to make him swift and strong. She remembered watching those muscles while they made love, thrusting their power outward, collapsing back in order to replenish the juice driving them.

For a long time, Megan relived the time she had spent with Carl. His movements, his words surrounded her, warming her. The icy cold subsided into a wet summer chill.

"Take my death," she whispered as she recalled his scent and invaded his pores with her pain.

Chirps. She heard birds. The patter of the rain was gone. Instead she could sense the heat of the sun, steaming away the preceding downpour. With a deep breath, she smelled the dampness of the soil beneath her.

She realized with that lungful of air there was no pain. Nothing prevented her from moving her hands to her face. She wiped away the water that had puddled into the crevices with the back of her hands. When she opened her eyes, the glare of the sun forced her to cover them with the shading of her palms.

Megan sat up and looked at the debris in front of her. All that was left of the house was a portion of the bedroom. The French doors remained open on singed hinges. The rest of the house was a blackened heap; smoke rose lightly from some minor fires. Megan was left to assume that among the debris was Beverly.

She turned to the grave and saw the knife on top of the mound, glinting in the sun. Her blood had been washed off it by the torrent of rain that had fallen. Instinctively, Megan touched her chest, feeling several long rips in her shirt. She expected the material to be enmeshed inside her chest cavity, but, dripping wet, it only lay flatly against her breast.

Dare she look down at the damage that was done? Her torso stiffened, and her head bobbed down as she tore the holes wider. The wounds were red and crusted. Scabs were fast healing; still, she was certain they would leave scars.

Megan ripped her shirt open, pulling the material down off her shoulders, comparing one breast to the other, the left a carved, mangled chunk of meat, with ribbons of welts crisscrossing, the right still whole, untouched.

After pulling the shirt back up and folding the material delicately across, trying to cover up, she laughed. How could she worry about decency? No one around there seemed to give any thought to the word.

When she stood, she felt a little light-headed. After she took in several deep breaths, it hit her. The smell of hyacinth was gone. Megan turned around to see that the hyacinth bushes had wilted and the flowers had fallen from the stems. Petals lay scattered on the ground. The leaves were a golden brown, and the stems looked almost like dry twigs. Perhaps the storm had been too much for the plant, or perhaps lightning . . . What did rational thinking get her? She would rather believe that they died of sorrow after their mistress had taken her own life. This sounded as good as anything else, after all that had happened.

Megan looked around for the journal. It was still under the garden swing beneath the elm, a bit drenched, but she hoped that the cover had managed to keep the pertinent writings dry. The shovel, which she tripped over, she would leave behind. Carl wouldn't need it anymore.

Megan was tempted to cross the threshold and enter the bedroom, but what good would it do? She would never know what Beverly had known, nor would she want to have that experience. Beverly had saved her from that, at least.

With a last lingering look at the French doors, Megan sped away from the rubble and headed down to the rowboat. She wondered whether Carl was looking for her. Would he have noticed the boat was gone? Would he have guessed where she went?

Knowing that she was able to continue on her way safely with the journal lying near her feet gave her the courage once again to face Carl. He wouldn't be able to destroy her the way he had Beverly. Besides, she needed provisions. A lie, she admitted. She could find a town soon enough and get help. But she didn't want to reveal what had occurred, fearing how people would react.

The boat drew closer to the landing, which was not far from Carl's house. The house was invisible behind the full summer foliage. Her feet splashed into the water, and she dragged the small vessel up onto the land. This time it was unnecessary to upend the boat, since the sky was clear.

Midway down the path she heard heavy huffing. Turning off into the bushes, Megan came upon Carl, shoulder deep in a hole from which he was pitching dirt. *Damn, he has another shovel,* she cursed. Quietly she drew closer. On the ground behind Carl's naked back sat a drawing. Her feet inched toward it. It was perfect. It was like looking into a mirror. Her hand shot out to grab it, but Carl turned and she was hypnotized by the change in him.

His cheeks were sunken, his skin mottled with grayish shadings. The eyelids sagged over a filmy blue, and the blond was gone from his hair, leaving thinning gray strands. His lungs heaved out heavy breaths from a concave chest and his muscles were frail, throbbing, tight balls.

"My God!" he shouted.

Then she knew that he had seen her wounds.

"What happened?" His voice quivered.

Megan looked again at the drawing. It would have been a perfect creation before this morning. Now it was useless to Carl. Her hand, which had been frozen in her reach, dropped back to her side.

The air lacked the sweet hyacinth scent; instead, it smelled putrid, like something starting to go bad. Like meat decaying on a hot summer afternoon. Megan glanced down at Carl with a smile on her face.

She left Carl calling out to her and went up to the house to collect her belongings. She took as much of the food as she needed. Carl would probably no longer have any use for it.

By the time she returned to the middle of the path, there was an old, stooped man waiting there. He had no shirt, and his pants hung loosely over withering hips.

"You have to tell me what happened. Where did you go? I couldn't find the boat. I looked for you. The house! You went to the house, didn't you?" Carl reached out to grab Megan's shoulders. She easily pushed away his weakened hands. Detouring around him was not difficult, since he had none of his agility left. Obviously he was much too stunned to reason out clearly what action to take.

"You promised not to leave me. At least not until the summer was over. Please come back."

Megan heard the shuffle of tired feet traveling behind her, but she outdistanced him and had already set the boat adrift when he tried to rest his hand on her arm.

"I'm ill, Megan. Please help me. I don't want to die." A phlegmy cough forced him to fall back. Once free, Megan threw her things inside the rowboat. Before jumping in, she turned to Carl.

His hands were shaking. He wouldn't be able to alter the drawing even if his memory was good enough to allow it. Megan jumped into the vessel, lifted the oars, clumping them into the water. Carl's tainted flesh looked dewy pale, covered with the river water that had been splashed on him. His head shook.

"No, Megan, please. Talk to me. Let me explain what's been happening. I don't know what Beverly told you, but listen to me. Believe me. Give me a chance to live. Don't let me die this way. Please, I'll waste away with the flies and maggots, and I can't prevent it, I can't stop it. Megan! Megan!"

Megan had pushed off, heading away from both the remains of the yellow house and Carl's home. Her arms seemed to build up strength with every push against the water.

At last, when she was out of earshot of Carl's voice, Megan rested the oars on the bottom of the boat. When she pulled out a fresh white cotton shirt and took off the old one, she was surprised how little blood spotted the shirt. The rain had managed to wash the cloth almost clean. She dumped the shirt into the water, letting it float atop the surface. Before putting on the new shirt, she checked the wounds. Already whitened scars were forming; the scabs had fallen off. She slipped on the new shirt and buttoned it right up to her neck, since she was self-conscious about the scars.

What would she tell Hester about her trip? Well, she had time to think about that. She was on her way home. No more woods and communing with the wilds of nature.

Chapter 43
Best Friend

"Hi, I'm home."

Megan heard Hester slam the door behind her. Hester had many flaws, but this was the one that most irritated Megan.

"You still studying?" Hester tossed her blazer over the canvas chair.

"Finishing up a paper."

"I don't know why you bothered to go to graduate school. Even I, the master of C grades, managed to land a decent position in a small company. You could have done better with your honors."

"Not with my major."

"I was a history major, medieval, mind you. You think that made me far more desirable in the eyes of the vast wasteland called Human Resources?"

"You were lucky."

"Not true. Talented and attractive? Yes." Hester started to remove her skirt. The mass of pleats fell to the floor. Hester daintily stepped out of the circle of material, and then, with the determination of a football kicker, she banished the skirt to a clump of clothes on the other side of the room. "By the way, whose turn is it to do the laundry?"

Megan pointed a finger at Hester, who wasn't buying it.

"I did it last week! Or did I? Let's see, I met that really cute CPA when I was trying to get that awful cranberry stain out of your blouse."

"Can't get cranberry out of anything."

"What do you mean? I did a pretty good job."

"Yeah. Now, instead of a stain, I have a hole in the blouse."

"A small hole. You cover it with a pretty pin, and no one will notice. Anyway, I think it's your turn this week. We really should make a chart, because I keep getting the impression that I'm starting to know the laundry custodian far better than you do."

"Maybe he likes you. Probably has a giant crush on black-eyed beauties."

"Just what I need, a sixty-year-old man with a potbelly, bald, and the mange creeping up his neck."

"It's a rash from shaving."

"Are you sure?"

Megan nodded, not lifting her eyes from the

pad she had been writing in before Hester had arrived.

"Looks like the mange to me. Why did you go to graduate school, anyway?" Hester asked as she wriggled out of her panty hose.

"I told you, I'm interested in anthropology, and now that Ma died, I have the cash to pay for classes. Besides, I couldn't get a decent job doing anything more interesting."

"It must have been a shock to find out your mother passed away while you were hiking in the woods. It's a good thing you decided to come home a month before schedule. By the way, have the lawyers cleared up her estate?"

"Yeah, she left that bozo she married the cat and the car; everything else is mine."

"Why the cat and car?"

"Because they bought both of them together. What was left of Dad's estate she left to me."

"The bozo must have been disappointed."

Megan shrugged. She didn't care how he felt.

Hester's 38-D breasts popped out of the brassiere after she unhooked the cloth in the back.

"It feels so good to get out of these work clothes."

"I've noticed. Every night you strip as soon as you come in the door. Someday I'll have a visitor, and you'll—"

"Megan, you never have company. All you ever do is read and write." Hester slipped the strings of her black bikini down over her hips and let the silk fabric drape over the tops of her feet. "You think my feet are too big?"

Megan looked at Hester's feet.

"Wait, I'll get rid of the bikini."

"Hester, that bikini is so small, it could never cover those boats."

"What?" Hester threw the silken fabric at Megan, who ducked, letting the garment fall behind her.

"I'm going to take a shower," Hester said.

"Must be a heavy date."

"What's that supposed to mean?"

"Just teasing."

Hester left the room as Megan watched. Hester's slender waist and hips swiveled exaggeratedly, and her sculpted rump quivered to the beat.

Megan had not told her roommate the true story for ending her vacation so soon, claiming simply that she had become lonely. She had meant to burn Carl's journal when she got back. It would be of little use to her. She had made the decision not to follow Carl's path. She would accept death when it caught up with her. Not knowing how long she had, she decided to go to graduate school. Maybe she could learn more about the tribe Carl had visited, but she didn't need the journal anymore, for she had taken her own notes on the tribe and where they were located. The journal should definitely be burned, so that no one else would be tempted, and yet she had not been able to do it. Instead she hid it in a safe-deposit box at her bank.

Hester stuck her head into the room. "By the way, if Frank calls, tell him he should be late, because I am."

"As always." Megan chuckled at the Bronx cheer Hester gave her.

There was a sudden pain in Megan's chest, sharp, affecting not only the internal organs but her skin as well. Megan's breath halted until the pain passed. Gradually she started to inhale, taking small, careful breaths. A portion of her left breast started to burn.

"What the heck?" Megan cautiously rose from the couch and went into the bedroom, where there was a full-length mirror behind the door. As she raised her arms to pull the T-shirt off, a stabbing pain crossed the left side of her chest.

"Damn," she swore as she gently guided the white cotton material over her head. She let the shirt fall from her hand as she gazed at her own reflection.

"Oh my God!" she cried.

The scars were reddening into welts. The transition back into wounds was beginning. How long would it take?

The pain had subsided, and she was able to use her arms freely again to slip the shirt back over her head and shoulders.

Was she really going to die? she wondered. It had happened over nine months ago. It had almost seemed like a nightmare, not a reality.

"Is something wrong?" she heard Hester call.

"No. Why?"

"I heard you cry out something."

"A pimple is starting on my chin."

"Bummer."

Yes, it certainly was. Megan stared into her own eyes and saw herself shining back from her pupils in the reflection. Then there was Beverly, with knife in hand, raising it to strike Megan. She remembered exactly how Beverly had looked. Would Megan die quickly from her wounds, or would she waste away like that?

Megan went back to the living room. Her pad and pencil were still on the couch. She picked them up, then dropped her rear down on the striped pillow.

Next month she may be nonexistent, lying next to her mother under that awful archangel her mother had bought when Dad had died. She recalled the white taffeta lining of her mother's coffin contrasting so garishly with the heavily made-up face, the cheeks puffed up with gauze. Too much gauze; her mother always had a well-defined bone structure with prominent cheekbones and hollow cheeks. The funeral director didn't know that. Her mother's bozo couldn't even locate a photograph to show the mortician. Would Hester whip out one of those ugly shots she had taken of Megan on their ski trip? Good Lord, who knows what she would look like lying in some pine box. Perhaps like Beverly. Her thoughts halted as images of the past summer months played back in her head. She would suffer the same slow living decay as the hyacinth woman. And then she would die. She would cease to exist.

Her right hand was working a pencil across a sheet of paper when Hester came into the room, wet and naked.

"No calls?"

Megan was silent.

"Yoo-hoo, Megan?"

She looked up, seeing the softness and contour of Hester's shape. Megan had always wondered at how light and downy Hester's body hair was, considering that Hester had a shiny black mane.

"When did you get that?" Megan asked, directing the point of her pencil toward Hester's right knee.

"Oh, it's nothing. I scraped my knee and kind of cut my palms," Hester said, raising her hands up so Megan could see, "while running up some stairs at work. Don't think I can collect workman's comp, though, do you?"

When Megan didn't laugh, Hester did.

"Gee, Megan, you're so serious. It's like living back home with my folks. You don't have to worry about my bruises. I'll be all right. Honest."

Realizing that she was making Hester uncomfortable, Megan tried to smile, but her eyes were so intent on taking in all the special physical qualities that made Hester who she was that it looked more like a grimace of pain.

"Are you all right, Megan?"

"Sure," she said, while her pencil stroked the paper swiftly.

Thank God, thought Megan, that I have a roommate who's so uninhibited.

HOWL-O-WEEN
Gary L. Holleman

Evil lurks on Halloween night....

H ear the demons wail in the night,
O ut of terror and out of fright,
W erewolves, witch doctors, and zombies too
L urk in the dark and wait for you.
O ther scary creatures dwell
W here they can drag you off to hell.
E vil waits for black midnight
E nchanting with magic and dark voodoo,
N ow Halloween has cast its spell.

_4083-2 $4.99 US/$5.99 CAN

Dorchester Publishing Co., Inc.
65 Commerce Road
Stamford, CT 06902

Please add $1.75 for shipping and handling for the first book and
$.50 for each book thereafter. NY, NYC, PA and CT residents,
please add appropriate sales tax. No cash, stamps, or C.O.D.s. All
orders shipped within 6 weeks via postal service book rate.
Canadian orders require $2.00 extra postage and must be paid in
U.S. dollars through a U.S. banking facility.

Name_____
Address_____
City _____ State _____Zip_____
I have enclosed $_____in payment for the checked book(s).
Payment <u>must</u> accompany all orders.☐ Please send a free catalog.

THE DARK DOOR
Kate Wilhelm

"Wilhelm is in top form as the thriller plot races along and the characters teeter over an abyss of insanity!"

—*Publishers Weekly*

Someone is setting fire to abandoned hotels, restaurants and schools around the country, at erratic intervals, and in apparently arbitrary locations. Worse, each time a building is torched, the arson is accompanied by madness, murder and mutilation. Charlie Meiklejohn and Constance Leidl will have to call upon all their skills to discover what lies behind this random insanity. What they will discover is far more terrifying than they can imagine....

_3416-6 $4.50 US/$5.50 CAN